"Where have you been?"

Kimberly whispered, trying to stay calm in front of the fourth graders gathered for a science demonstration.

"My experiment in chem lab exploded," Derek said. "I figured you could hold down the fort."

"I am going to hold down your head—preferably under water—if you ever flake out on me like this again."

A balloon whizzed past them, splatting against the chalkboard.

"I got all these future scientists here started," said Kimberly. "I think you'd better take over. I have some things of my own to take care of for tonight's performance."

"You're leaving me alone?"

"Toughen up, Weldon. It's only a room full of kids." A balloon zapped him in the head. "And remember, I expect to see you in the audience, eight o'clock sharp."

"I'll try to—"

"Don't try. Be there." She shook a fist at him. "Or you're going to experience Kimberly Dayton's personal law of action–reaction firsthand."

FRESHMAN FLING

LINDA A. COONEY

HarperPaperbacks
A Division of HarperCollinsPublishers

This is a work of fiction. The characters, incidents, and
dialogues are products of the author's imagination and are not
to be construed as real. Any resemblance to actual events or
persons, living or dead, is entirely coincidental.

HarperPaperbacks *A Division of* HarperCollins*Publishers*
10 East 53rd Street, New York, N.Y. 10022

Cover illustration by Tony Greco

First HarperPaperbacks printing: July 1991

Printed in the United States of America

HarperPaperbacks and colophon are trademarks of
HarperCollins*Publishers*

10 9 8 7 6 5 4 3 2 1

One

······················

Kimberly Dayton stood like a statue in the middle of Coleridge Hall's basement mail room. Other students on lunch break crowded in and out, laughing, shouting, and roughhousing, but Kimberly barely felt them push past her. She shoved the note she'd found in her mailbox deep into her dance bag and squeezed her slender body through the crowd to the door. She loved living in the creative arts dorm, but right now all she wanted was to get out.

Her long, dancer's legs carried her quickly and gracefully out of Coleridge and into the warm, spring air. University of Springfield students mobbed the huge, grassy rectangle surrounded by dorms. Kimberly walked among the Frisbee players, sunbathers, couples sharing blankets, friends eating lunch on the grass. How could their world seem so happy when hers was falling apart?

"Duck!" yelled a guy running right at her. Kimberly wanted to stand her ground and let the ball and the player ram into her; if she was injured she'd have a way out of her mess. Instead, Kimberly entered the flow of students leaving the green, heading toward the quad for their Thursday one o'clock classes.

"Kimberly! Kimberly, wait up!"

Kimberly turned, looking over the heads of the oncoming mob. A hand waved in the distance and a familiar blond braid swung from side to side. Kimberly smiled and waved back, waiting for Faith Crowley to catch up with her.

Faith, Kimberly's dorm neighbor, had been one of her first new friends on campus. And since Faith's two best friends practically lived in her dorm room, Kimberly had inherited Winnie Gottlieb and KC Angeletti as friends, too. "Thought . . . I saw . . . you in . . . the mail room," gasped Faith, clutching a jumble of textbooks, mail, and the new *Theatercrafts* magazine to her overalls.

"What's up?" asked Kimberly, hoping she didn't sound upset. Faith had antennae that picked up even the smallest problems.

"We have yet another new mail person at Coleridge Hall," said Faith, searching through her mail. "And not nearly as efficient as KC was. Here!" She pulled out an elegant, neatly addressed, tan envelope. "This was put into my mailbox by mistake. It looks important."

"Thanks," said Kimberly, barely looking at the envelope as she slipped it into her *Introduction to Physics* textbook.

"Aren't you going to open it?"

"It?" asked Kimberly. "Oh, the letter. Don't have to. I already know what it says."

"Kimberly, you can't know what a letter says before you read it."

Kimberly handed the letter to Faith. "Open it," she said, as the two girls walked together toward their classes.

Looking puzzled, Faith slipped her finger under the flap and opened the letter.

"The letter is neatly typed and one page long," Kimberly said.

"Right."

"In the upper right-hand corner is the date, the time of day, and the weather."

"April second, five P.M., sunny, fifty-seven degrees," read Faith.

"The first paragraph asks how my health is. The second paragraph tells me what's happening in Martin's life at Drake."

Faith scanned the letter. "You're right! Who's Martin?"

"The third paragraph," said Kimberly, ignoring the question, "asks me to write when I have time. The letter is signed . . ." she closed her eyes, trying to remember. "Let's see. The last one was signed 'Sincerely' so this one is signed 'Yours truly.' He alternates."

Faith whistled softly. "Are you psychic?"

"Hardly. Martin Frazier is the childhood friend my entire family expects me to marry. My grandmother cuts out magazine photos of wedding dresses she wants to sew for me. My aunt constantly reminds me Martin has the three B's."

"The three B's?" asked Faith. Kimberly sighed. Holding up three fingers, she counted them off one by one. "He's black," she said, "he's beautiful, and he's bright."

Faith smiled. "Now, why do I get the feeling you're not so happy about him?"

"He's also the fourth deadly B," said Kimberly. "Bor-ing. But try to convince my family of that."

"I know how you feel," said Faith, slipping the letter back into the envelope. "I broke up with Brooks months ago, but my family still asks about him in every letter. They really want me to still be with my high school boyfriend." As she handed the envelope back, her caring eyes searched Kimberly's face. "Is there something wrong?" she asked. "I mean, besides Mr. Bor-ing? You seem a little down."

"Well . . . I . . . I wasn't going to bother you. But . . ." The campus chimes rang, announcing the hour.

"Darn," said Faith. "I've got to run; got a quiz. Come to my room tonight. My folks sent an emergency shipment of chocolate chip cookies. We'll talk then." She darted toward the English building. "Everything looks better over a chocolate chip cookie," she called back over her shoulder.

"I'll be there."

Faith disappeared and Kimberly turned into the Math and Science building. It would be a relief to talk to a friend about the pale-green note in her dance bag. Faith would understand how a harmless-looking piece of paper could drop like a bomb into Kimberly's life. Faith was always so willing to listen, so eager to help. Maybe, between the two of them, they'd think of some way out of this mess.

Kimberly climbed the stairs to the third floor three at a time. This new building was so different from the dance center where she spent most of her time. There, the pine floor planks and oak-paneled walls echoed the sounds of music and laughter, dancing feet, and teacher's instructions. This building sucked up sound like a black hole. A person could disappear in a building like this, and that is just what Kimberly wanted to do.

The physics classroom filled quickly. Kimberly slid onto her stool at the lab table. Everywhere around the room were pieces of equipment designed to do something. This was a place of creation—just like a dance studio was. Sometimes science excited Kimberly every bit as much as dance. If only she could make her mother understand that.

"Got any extra paper?" asked the girl across from her. "I forgot my notebook."

"Sure," said Kimberly. She lifted her notebook from her dance bag and passed the girl a few sheets of paper. The pale-green note glared from inside the bag. Kimberly knew it by heart.

Miss Dayton,

I have selected three of my freshman students to perform in the dance portion of the
upcoming *Week at the U* concert. Your delight-
ful "Magician at Midnight" is scheduled third
on the final Wednesday night program. Congratulations!
Ms. Zarkin.

Congratulations? Obviously Ms. Zarkin
thought she was doing Kimberly a favor, but what
she'd really done was strike terror in Kimberly's
heart. The *Week at the U* was the university's most
important week of the year. Every day, from next
Wednesday through the following Wednesday, ten
different events would be sponsored by ten different university groups. Prospective students,
alumni, politicians, media, everyone who was anyone would come to watch or participate. Atten-
dance was always very high.

"Anyone have the chem notes from last Friday?"
someone asked.

"Whose lab?"

"McMillan's."

"I do," said a girl in back. "You can copy mine,
but I need them back by the end of class."

Kimberly took out her pens and highlighters

and set them on the desk. How could Ms. Zarkin do this to her? "Magician at Midnight" was never meant to be performed. It was just something Kimberly had been choreographing for her Modern Dance class. If she could barely get up enough nerve to dance in front of a handful of fellow students, how was she supposed to perform in front of several hundred people?

"Good afternoon, class." As usual, Professor Jobst raced in just after the bell. "Everyone find a seat, please," he said, hurriedly erasing the board full of notes he'd scrawled during his morning Beginning Physics class. This hour, he'd write the same notes all over again for Kimberly's class. Some people hated doing things over and over, but not Kimberly.

From the time she was a toddler, she'd spent most of her days at the dance studios where her mother rehearsed her company, the Houston Modern Dance Troupe. Kimberly could practice in the studios for hours and hours on end. She danced when she was happy. She danced when she was sad. She danced and danced when there was no reason to dance except for the sheer joy of moving her body to music.

"Magician at Midnight" had started that way. Kimberly had gone with Faith, Winnie, and KC to see Walt Disney's *Fantasia* and had become fascinated by Paul Duka's haunting score for "The Sorcerer's Apprentice." Ever since, she had been inspired to create steps evoking a sorcerer's magical powers.

"For the next two sessions," said Prof. Jobst, "we will explore Isaac Newton's third law of motion."

Kimberly turned to a fresh page in her notebook and wrote: "Newton—third law of motion," neatly highlighting the words in yellow. As the professor talked, she skipped a line and copied his words: "For every action, there is an equal and opposite reaction." *That's for sure,* she thought.

Action: go up on stage.

Reaction: throw up from fear.

Kimberly sighed. Working at the barre or leaping across a mirrored room was not the same as getting up on a stage in front of an audience. *Week at the U* was bigger than big, huger than huge, and Ms. Zarkin wanted to plunk Kimberly smack dab in the middle of it. Kimberly couldn't do it. She'd tried performing in front of an audience once this year, only to end up paralyzed by stage fright backstage. It terrified her to think of trying again.

Kimberly smiled, drawing musical notes around the border of the page. That probably wasn't the action-reaction Newton had in mind, but Kimberly liked physics. So much of it was the study of movement in space, and in that way it was similar to dance.

"Miss Dayton?"

"Yes?"

"If you would."

Her heart thudded as Prof. Jobst waved her up. She felt the eyes of her classmates watching her walk to the front of the room. The professor often used students in his physics demonstrations but Kimberly had been lucky enough to avoid being picked so far. She needn't have worried. Prof. Jobst simply asked her to reach into the "team box" and pull out a piece of paper on which was written a classmate's name. Each pair of students was to work on a project exploring action and re-action. Derek Weldon was the name Kimberly pulled.

"Excuse me, Prof. Jobst," she said, walking up to the teacher after class, "but I don't know who Derek Weldon is."

"Ah, yes. Derek asked permission to transfer out of my morning class into this one. I believe he had a conflict in his schedule with some activity or other. He was supposed to be here today. I'll find out what happened and have him contact you."

Just what I need, a flaky physics partner. If Derek Weldon couldn't make it to class, Kimberly probably couldn't count on him to help her put together a decent project. She slung her bag over her shoulder and trotted down the stairs.

Well, she'd do the project, even if she had to work on it alone. At least it would take her mind off the *Week at the U,* and having to dance in front of 500 people. She shuddered. There had to be a way out of this.

Two

· · · · · · · · · · · · · · · · ·

"Please, please, *please,* don't let me eat any more cookies!" Faith moaned, unsnapping the sides of her overalls.

"Same goes for me," said KC, rolling her large, gray eyes and running her fingernails through her long, black hair. She sat on the dorm room's only uncluttered chair, her patent leather shoes and leather briefcase tucked neatly underneath. "Thank goodness your parents didn't send cookies before I posed for the Classic Calendar," she said, referring to the campus calendar featuring the most beautiful men and women at U of S. KC's stunning photograph had turned her into a campus celebrity. She picked a couple of cookie crumbs off her pleated skirt and placed them on a napkin. "No one would want to include me in the calendar today. I think I just put on fifty pounds."

"Then I must've put on sixty," said Kimberly, whose maroon Flexitard and navy tights followed the finely toned muscles of her dancer's body. She stretched her long legs slowly into a split. "I feel like the "before" photo in one of those weight-loss ads."

"You sure don't look it," said Faith. "If I were five-foot ten, I could eat everything I wanted." She groaned. "Even my braid feels fat."

"The trick," said Winnie, her jumble of plastic bracelets clicking as she reached for yet another cookie, "is to do ten bent-knee sit-ups and ten push-ups after each cookie." Hooking the toes of her neon sneakers under Faith's bed, she somehow managed to eat cookies, do sit-ups, and study from the open psychology book at her side, all at the same time. "Plus, of course, promising yourself to run one mile for every cookie you eat."

"*Now* you tell us," said Faith. "That means I'll have to run to Florida and back."

She smiled, feeling wonderfully content. What a treat it was to have her best friends gathered in her room. She'd grown up with Winnie and KC in

Jacksonville, a small, Western town. Best friends since eighth grade, they were now at U of S together, but they didn't live in the same dorm, and were no longer inseparable. Winnie was always going off in a million wacky directions; KC, the most serious of their group, was busy pledging Tri Beta, the most exclusive sorority on campus; and Faith was involved with project after project for the theater department. Their schedules had become so hectic that times like these came fewer and farther apart. So Faith appreciated having a good friend living right next door. Even though Kimberly hadn't grown up with them, her easy humor and concern for others fit right in with their group.

"If I explode," said Kimberly, bouncing gently into a split to stretch her hamstrings, "just scrape me off the walls."

"Don't explode on these walls!" cried Faith. "You'll splatter all over Liza's photos."

Photos of Liza Ruff, Faith's frizzy red-haired new roommate, covered half the room's walls. This worried Faith, who suspected additional photographs would slowly creep onto her half. Faith was too nice to say anything; she just accepted the fact that Liza, who had a big mouth and an ego to match, loved being in the spotlight as much as her old roommate, Lauren Turnbell-Smythe, had hated it.

KC frowned. "Lauren would never have plastered publicity photos, composite sheets, and press clips of herself all over the room."

"I know," said Faith. "If anything, Lauren would have put up posters urging people to help the homeless, feed the hungry, and love thy neighbor."

"How is Lauren these days?" asked Kimberly. "I haven't seen her much since she moved off campus."

"Lauren's fine," said Faith. "She's really busy covering stories for the campus paper. I guess that means we won't see much of her until after *Week at the U.*"

"And where is your new roomie?" asked Winnie.

"Liza went home for three days to pick up the rest of her things. It's been absolute heaven not to have her following me around like a shadow." Faith looked at Liza's side of the room and shook her head glumly. "I just know that all the stuff she's bringing back is going to flow over her side of the room onto mine."

"Then pour it right back," said Winnie, matter-of-factly.

"I couldn't do that," said Faith.

"That's your problem," Winnie said. "You're too nice."

"She's right," said KC. "Anyone but you would have had ten different fights with Liza by now." She poured an instant cocoa packet into her cup and carefully added steaming water from Faith's electric kettle.

"Liza reminds me of my youngest sister," said Kimberly, leaning forward into her split. "They're both so spoiled that they think the whole universe revolves around them."

"If Liza had moved into my room," said Winnie, "I would have torn her red hair out by its black roots by now."

"I've given up studying in this room," said Faith. "Trying to read while Liza's around is like trying to study in a hurricane."

"But this is your room, too," said KC, who had rented a single room in an all-girl study dorm to avoid problems like these. "You have rights."

"I don't want to make trouble. I'll just keep looking for quiet places to hide out in."

"I've got it!" said Winnie. She jumped up and stood in the center of the room. "Remember those two sisters in middle school, the ones who were always fighting?"

"The Mishmush girls," said KC. She clapped

her hands and laughed. "I haven't thought about them in years."

"I remember!" said Faith.

"The what?" Kimberly asked.

"That was what the three of us called them," explained Faith. "The Mishmush girls were at school with us from third to sixth grade. They were French and we couldn't pronounce their real name. Mishmush was as close as we got."

"And they fought all the time," said Winnie. "About everything."

"Winnie," Faith said, "what on earth do the Mishmush girls have to do with me and Liza?"

"Remember what they did in their bedroom to protect one side from the other?" KC and Faith shook their heads. Winnie rummaged through the old fishing tackle box where Faith kept her theater supplies, and took out a piece of stage-marking chalk. She drew a line down the center of the floor, up the wall and, standing on the dresser, ran the line out onto the ceiling.

"Winnie—" Faith said, shaking her head, but there was no stopping Winnie when she got going.

By the time Winnie finished, she'd cut the room in half. "Now, everything on this side of the room is yours, and that side is Liza's," Winnie said. "If she hangs, drops, or tosses one single little thing on your side, you can jump on her nose until she takes it back."

"Thank you so much," said Faith, rescuing the chalk and wondering if she'd be able to erase the line before Liza came back.

Just then a loud voice in the hallway caused all the girls to look up. "Extra! Extra!" The voice belonged to the resident advisor, who stood at the door with a stack of flyers. As if her voice wasn't enough to get their attention, she also played a few quick notes on a bugle.

"Music major," explained Faith.

"Figures," said Winnie.

"Read all about the *Week at the U.*" The R.A. tossed each girl a colorful sheet. "Ten events a day for a whole week. Extra!" She blew the bugle again and went on to the next room.

Winnie, Faith, and KC scanned the list of events excitedly. Kimberly finished her stretches, leaned against the bed, and picked up a program.

"Oh, no!" she cried, pointing to the bottom of the sheet. "Here I am. Under the final Wednesday night dance program. " 'Magician at Midnight,' choreographed and danced by Miss Kimberly Dayton.' Now I'll *have* to perform!"

Faith listened as she dotted her steaming cocoa

with tiny marshmallows. She still felt guilty for insisting Kimberly star in The Follies, a talent show she had directed. How was she supposed to know that the outgoing, vivacious Kimberly who was always laughing, prancing, kidding around, would become paralyzed by stage fright? Faith couldn't let Kimberly suffer that horrible embarrassment again. She handed the cup to Kimberly.

"Thanks," said Kimberly, sliding her legs under her and sipping the hot cocoa. "I'd appreciate ideas any of you might have that will help me get through this *Week at the U.*"

"You could break a leg," said Winnie. "Then they couldn't make you dance."

"That would do it," said Kimberly. "But I was hoping for something a little less extreme."

"Winnie's always extreme," said Faith, rubbing her hand over Winnie's short, spiky hair. "If you think it will help," she went on, "I'll come watch you rehearse. It might give us an idea of what to do."

"Would you?" Kimberly blew out a sigh of relief. "That'd be great. I have a feeling I'm going to need all the help I can get."

"Darn, darn, double-darn," said Winnie, shaking her head over the flyer. "I want to go to all these programs! I'll never be able to choose."

"The film department is scheduling a great foreign film every night," said Faith. She ran her finger down the long list. "Science demonstrations, programs for children, a fencing exhibition—"

"Fencing?" said Kimberly. "That was my sport in high school. I've got to go see it."

"I'll go with you," said Faith. "I used to love pirate movies because of the great dueling scenes. My teacher says realistic-looking dueling scenes are hard to direct. I'd love to see fencing done in real life."

"The best were *The Three Musketeers,* " said KC.

"Friends banding together to fight evil," said Kimberly, using her spoon to make a dramatic swirl. "Touché!"

"Personally," said Winnie, "I liked Robin Hood and his band of merry men." She clasped her hands to her breast. "All that taking from the rich and giving to the poor. My kind of dude."

"That's a must, then," said Faith, circling fencing with her thick, black marker. "We'll all go and learn how to make the world safe from pirates."

"I wish I could," said KC. "But I'll only be able to make a few of the *Week's* events. My classes are snowing me under, and Tri Beta has all pledges working to get the sorority ready for our open house."

"Annnnnd?" said Winnie, wiggling her eyebrows.

"And what?" asked KC.

"Annnnnd, you didn't mention Peter Dvorsky in that looooong list of activities." She slid off one bracelet and held it over her eye like a camera. "Seems to me a certain photographer has been taking up an awful lot of your time."

"Not so much," said KC, her face turning beetred as she furiously studied the events sheet. "Oh, look, this lecture on international economics should be interesting."

"Gag," said Winnie.

"Sounds like a laugh a minute," said Kimberly, yawning.

"Unfortunately," KC said, "it's scheduled at the same time as fencing. I won't be able to go with you."

"Well, I'm definitely going to the fencing demonstration," said Faith. "And to every other event that doesn't conflict with a class. *Anything* to keep me out of this room."

"You should never have made Liza a star," said Winnie.

"I didn't. I made her Kimberly's understudy. And I only did that because Liza was so mad at me for not giving her a part in The Follies. I thought

Liza would be so busy learning Kimberly's song-and-dance routine that she'd stay out of my hair. I never meant for her to perform. I mean, understudies almost never get to go on stage."

"Except," said Kimberly, sympathetically, "when the featured performer gets stage fright."

"And," said Winnie, talking into an imaginary microphone, "as our hapless Kimberly stood frozen in the wings, understudy Liza Ruff jumped onto the stage and in a frenzy of off-key singing and comic dancing, saved the day. The Follies was a hit, director Faith Crowley was a hero, and Liza was a star."

"Go ahead, make fun," said Faith, "but since then Liza's been clinging to me like a second skin. She even transferred into my section of Acting 101. I think I liked it better when she didn't talk to me. I don't know how much more of this I can take."

Suddenly, a duffel bag sailed through the open door, crashed against the far wall, and dropped like a shot bird onto Liza's bed. Faith looked up, startled, shrinking back as Liza jumped into the doorway, her Bozo-red hair back-combed into a wild mane, her wide eyes bugging out, her yellow-and-black striped sweatsuit making her look like a horror film version of a giant bumblebee.

"And now, ladies and gents," shouted the familiar foghorn voice, "preeeee-zent-ing the one, the only, Liza Ruff, starring in her new role as Queen of the Dorm Rats. Co-starring," she whisked into the room and spread her arms wide, "Winnie the Skinny, Kimberly the Limberly, KC the . . ." She paused, with a funny look on her face. "What rhymes with KC? No matter."

Faith felt her nice, quiet world shatter into a thousand pieces. Liza twirled around to face her. "And the one, the only, the magnificent Keep-the-Faith Crowley, director extraordinaire, who turns straw into gold, molehills into mountains, and freshmen into stars. Especially," she bowed, "very talented freshmen with fabulous red hair." She threw her arms around Faith, hugging her like a long-lost sister instead of someone she'd seen just a few days ago.

Faith held her breath until Liza finally let go. Then she watched open-mouthed as Liza grabbed a few chocolate chip cookies, opened her duffel, and started unpacking. From the looks of all the stuff Liza brought, Faith had the sinking feeling Hurricane Liza was not likely to blow over soon.

Three

·····················

The next day, Winnie squinted against the bright sun as she stepped out of the between-classes traffic to wait for her friends. She tucked her western civ book under her arm and dug through her huge bag for her over-sized, neon sunglasses. *It was a magnificent day, a day of possibilities, a day when anything could happen,* she thought.

"It's just not fair," she said as her friends came out of the building.

"Our pop quiz?" asked KC, buttoning her blazer.

"That, too." Winnie put on her sunglasses and

gazed longingly across the quad to the mountains. "It's not fair to have to sit in a classroom on such a glorious day."

Faith cupped her hand to her mouth like a director's megaphone. "Bring back the sleet," she commanded. "Pile up the snow again until Winnie Gottlieb gets out for summer vacation."

"Speak for yourself," said Lauren, tightening her scarf under her chin. "I for one am grateful not to have to huddle around my tiny space heater for warmth." She pulled her army jacket around her. "My apartment is one part wall and nine parts draft."

"I vote we lock Liza in the closet," said Winnie, "and give you your old bed back."

"Don't tempt me," said Faith. "Yesterday she played her *Les Misérables* tape for ten hours straight. Arrrrgggghhhhh!"

"Let's run away to the mountains," said Winnie, looking off into the distance. "Can't you hear them calling our name?" She held a hand to her ear. "Winnnn-eeeee. Faiiiiith. Come climb, come run, come have a snowball fight. We're waiiiiiiit-ing."

"That's not the mountains," said Lauren, checking her watch. "That's my journalism teacher calling Laurrrr-en, hurry, or you'll be late again. Gotta go."

"I'll walk with you," Faith said, hoisting her bookbag over her shoulder. "I have to stop off at the theater. Besides, the least you can do is let me complain about the latest awful thing Liza has done."

With no classes to go to next period, Winnie and KC strolled, enjoying the brief break in their busy schedules.

"How's the sorority?" asked Winnie. "Still enjoying it?"

"I know it must sound weird," said KC, "but I really am."

"Hey, don't apologize for something that makes you happy." Winnie rested her hand on her friend's arm and squeezed it gently. "It's great that you're having a good time, KC. We all think so. You've always worked the hardest of all of us. It's about time you had a little fun."

"It's just that, well, you and Faith always made so much fun of the sorority girls."

"Things change," said Winnie. "Isn't that why we're here? To be open to new experiences? That's what my mom says. Weird, huh? What's even weirder is my classmates figure that because my mom's a psychologist, I know everything about the psyche."

"Like people coming into my parent's health-food restaurant expect me to know how to cook a tofu omelet," KC said. "I mean, really. Would they expect a plumber's kid to fix plumbing?"

The girls laughed, stopping at the place where the walk divided into two smaller paths. KC shifted her briefcase to her other hand and checked her watch. "I'd better get over to Tri Beta. Today's my day to clean the mail cubbies."

"Sounds gross," Winnie said.

"Yeah. Now you know what you're missing," KC said, as she headed off toward Tri Beta. "See you."

Winnie walked on toward her dorm. The delicious feeling of something-is-about-to-happen washed over her again. She smiled to herself and when she saw a rainbow from a sunbeam reflecting off the water in Plotsky Fountain, Winnie took it as an omen.

This is the day Winnie and Josh will finally get their romance back on track.

Winnie started jogging toward Forest Hall—toward Josh Gaffey. *Please let Josh be in his room. Please let us finally be alone,* Winnie prayed. Her stomach flipped at the thought of Josh, the bright, quirky computer major who lived down the hall from her. So far, their relationship had been plagued by misunderstandings, but Winnie was sure all they needed was time together in order to clear things up. And today was going to be the day. She could feel it. The rainbow was a sign if ever she saw one.

Winnie ran faster, thinking *Please let Josh be in his room. Please keep away nosy neighbors, studying roommates, midterm papers, dumb dorm pranks, and all the other ghoulies and gremlins that might keep me from being alone with Josh.*

Winnie stopped outside Forest Hall, catching her breath, jogging in place to warm down. *The hotline. How am I going to tell Josh about that call of his to the hotline?* she thought. Winnie bent down, stretching out her back leg muscles. She'd wait until their shaky relationship was on solid ground before she confessed that she was the one who had taken his call to the Crisis Hotline.

"I love this girl," he'd said, "and I don't know how I'm going to live without her." He'd poured his heart out about the girl he loved who'd gone back to her old boyfriend. He hadn't given his name, but Winnie had recognized Josh's voice. Only her volunteer's oath of confidentiality kept her from telling him it was her, that she loved him, too, and had sent the old boyfriend away. She had to tell him soon, just not now. Not yet.

Please let him be home, please let him be home, please
. . . Winnie stood outside the door to room 141, Josh's room. She pressed her fingertips against the door and closed her eyes. Concentrating with all her might, she willed Josh to be inside. Finally, she knocked. The door flung open.

"Hi!" she said as cheerfully as she could.

Josh looked awful. Dark bags sagged under his bleary eyes, his face was shadowed by beard stubble, and his tangle of dark hair looked like it hadn't seen a comb for days.

"Oh," he said, surprised. Then he smiled and Winnie thought she'd never seen anyone more handsome. "Hi, yourself. Come in. But be careful. He nodded at the piles of papers strewn all over the floor. "I've been working all night on this project. I nearly had it nailed down when some joker hit the main switch and shut down the power. I lost three hours work off the computer."

"Oh, Josh. How awful."

He bent over the papers, rummaging through

one stack, then another, picking some papers up, leaving others, then stuffing a batch into his knapsack.

"It's my own fault," he said, talking as fast as he moved. "I've been meaning to get a computer program that would automatically save my work every few minutes. My dad says I'm always closing the barn door *after* the horse runs away. I've got to start doing things when I think of doing them. Before it's too late."

Winnie walked up to him, wanting to kiss him and hug him and cuddle with him for the rest of the day. "How about listening to music for a while," Winnie suggested. "You look like you could use a break."

"Sorry, Win. I wish I could." He jammed his bare foot into moccassins and closed the zipper on his knapsack. "I've got to get to the computer lab. A guy there has data that will cut my work time in half. If I don't stop to sleep or eat for the next two days, I should finish my project by my Monday afternoon class."

Winnie watched helplessly as he looked around for anything else he might have missed, then grabbed his keys. Another chance for them to be alone was slipping by.

"Wait," she said, leaning back against the door, blocking it to stop him from leaving.

"Gotta get going, Winnie."

"You can't go until I know when I'll see you next. Let's make a date, set a time, pick a place." Her motor mouth was going full speed, because she knew she wouldn't be able to study, to think, to *breathe* if they didn't make a date this very second.

Josh walked up to her, pressing his nose to hers, crossing his eyes. "There are four of you," he said. Winnie laughed. He kissed the tip of her nose. "Don't stop me now," he said, "or I'll never get my work done. Then I'll flunk out and you'll never see me again."

Winnie's mind raced. "Let's plan to meet for lunch on Tuesday," she said. "Your project will be finished, and you'll have caught up on your sleep."

"Can't. I have computer graphics at one." He kissed her left cheek.

"What about in the morning then?" she asked.

"Morning?" Josh kissed her right cheek.

She reached up and brushed a lock of hair off his forehead. "Yes, morning. You know, when the sun comes up and chases away the dark."

"Sun?" he asked. Josh was not a morning person.

"Josh." Winnie threatened him with a hard look.

"Okay," he said, his eyes at half mast. "I have no classes that morning."

"Me either," said Winnie. "So the way I figure it, we'll meet right after breakfast."

"Your place or mine?"

"My room's out," Winnie said. "I think my roommate is glued to her desk chair. The only time Melissa leaves is to eat, see her boyfriend, or go to class. What about your room? Will Mikoto be there Tuesday morning?"

Josh smiled. "My roomy, unlike yours, lives in the pre-med library," he said. He kissed the right corner of Winnie's mouth. "I think he's set up a cot in the corner." He kissed the left corner. "Only comes here to change underwear and beat me at computer games." He put a finger under her chin and tilted her head up, bringing his lips to hers.

The world slipped away. Winnie closed her eyes and felt herself fall into the warmth of his lips, the tenderness of his kiss.

Josh pulled away. "If I don't get to the computer lab right now I'm going to flunk this course." Winnie pouted, sticking out her lower lip. Josh laughed. "Don't sulk. I don't like this any more than you do. I promise I'll meet you Tuesday, bright and early."

Winnie tapped a tiny fist against his chest. "And remember not to make any plans for next Saturday night. We'll go to the All Dorm Pizza Party together."

"Whazzat?"

Winnie nuzzled his chest. "Our dorm is sponsoring a pizza party, remember? Part of *Week at the U.*"

"Never heard of it."

"Saturday night, Josh. Next Saturday night."

"What about the Saturday night after that?"

Winnie looked up at him. He was smiling at her with that wonderful impish look he got when he was teasing. "Yes, the following Saturday night, too," she said, chills running up and down her whole body. "And the Saturday night after that. You'll never get rid of me."

She felt his strong arms around her, hugging her, and his soft lips kissing her over and over and over.

"I've really got to get out of here," he said, pulling back, his eyes misty from lack of sleep and from being in love.

"All right," said Winnie, reluctantly moving

away from the door. "But I'll see you Tuesday morning."

"It's a date," said Josh, kissing her quickly one last time before he raced out the door and down the stairs.

racefully down the front stairs. The
long silk scarf she'd tossed around her
out behind her. KC beamed at the
. She could still hardly believe that of
es to choose from, Tri Beta's president
her out as a friend.
stood on the last step and clapped her
times. "Attention, please, everyone."
or the pledges to quiet down. The sun
from the window at the top of the
d through her blond hair. Courtney
hands again. "I need you all in the
for a quick meeting," she said.
leave our stuff here?" someone asked.
ly done."
d Courtney. "This won't take long."
d the dash to the living room, flopping
the others on the thick rug. "Oh, no,"
tly, looking at her shoes. The cleaning
splashed on her patent leather pumps
ittle, round holes through the finish.
by far her most comfortable pair, were

shame," said Marcia Tabbert next to
saw a pair just like those last week at
es. I'm sure they still have them."
" said KC, trying to smile. There was

Four

....

"**H**as anyone seen the green marker?"
"We've got it over here!" A thick,
green marker sailed across the Tri
Beta foyer, barely missing KC's bucket.

Beautifully dressed pledges huddled on the floor
around KC, noisily working on their art projects
while KC cleaned out the mail cubbies. One group
was putting together a collage of sorority activities, while another was assembling a poster tracing
Tri Beta's history. "Evita" played on the living
room disc player, and a group upstairs practiced
new harmony for Tri Beta songs.

"I think this *Week at the U* is a dumb idea,"

grumbled the pledge next to KC. KC couldn't remember the girl ever being happy about anything. "I have better things to do than glue construction paper on poster board."

"It's only one week," said KC. "It'll be over soon."

This girl could never be KC's friend. She had a selfish streak in her, like Marielle Danner, the Tri Beta whose mean tricks had made KC depledge during the first semester. Marielle had been kicked out, and Courtney Conner the Tri Beta president had asked KC to give the sorority one more chance. KC had to admit that, between her activities in Tri Beta and her growing romance with Peter, these last few weeks had been her happiest since she came to U. of S.

Diane Woo, Tri Beta's beautiful and efficient secretary, walked into the foyer wearing body-hugging cycling gear, her feather-light racing bike balanced on her shoulder. Her face had a healthy glow from a long workout. "How's it going, ladies?" she asked.

"Fine," chorused the pledges.

"Great. Try to finish up. We're going to have a meeting in a few minutes and I want to clear the foyer. Hey, KC," she said, smiling as she passed. "Those cubbies are looking mighty fine."

"Thanks," said KC, pr
done.

"How'd you get stuck w
"I volunteered."
"You're kidding!"
"It's sort of fun cleaning
said KC. "Like raking a y;
or washing a mud-caked c;
Diane was that she could
posters. One drop of ne
indelible marker, could r
her sorority sisters, she co
out and replace a ruined
ents were already struggl
and at the moment, KC
job.

"Anybody see the glue
"One more minute. W
"We've got tape over h
"No, gotta have glue."
KC's hands burned ev
into the bucket; the cle
too strong for her sensi
red and raw. "Done,"
around the last cubby. S
her work.

"Looks great, KC,"

she sai
ends of
neck fl
complir
all the p
had sin;

Cour
hands a
She wait
streamin
stairs fil
clapped
living ro
"Can
"We're n
"Yes,"
KC joi
down wi
she said
solvent h
and eate
The shoe
ruined.

"That's
her. "But
Vogue Sl
"Thank

Four
....

"**H**as anyone seen the green marker?"

"We've got it over here!" A thick, green marker sailed across the Tri Beta foyer, barely missing KC's bucket.

Beautifully dressed pledges huddled on the floor around KC, noisily working on their art projects while KC cleaned out the mail cubbies. One group was putting together a collage of sorority activities, while another was assembling a poster tracing Tri Beta's history. "Evita" played on the living room disc player, and a group upstairs practiced new harmony for Tri Beta songs.

"I think this *Week at the U* is a dumb idea,"

grumbled the pledge next to KC. KC couldn't re-member the girl ever being happy about anything. "I have better things to do than glue construction paper on poster board."

"It's only one week," said KC. "It'll be over soon."

This girl could never be KC's friend. She had a selfish streak in her, like Marielle Danner, the Tri Beta whose mean tricks had made KC depledge during the first semester. Marielle had been kicked out, and Courtney Conner the Tri Beta president had asked KC to give the sorority one more chance. KC had to admit that, between her activities in Tri Beta and her growing romance with Peter, these last few weeks had been her happiest since she came to U. of S.

Diane Woo, Tri Beta's beautiful and efficient secretary, walked into the foyer wearing body-hugging cycling gear, her feather-light racing bike balanced on her shoulder. Her face had a healthy glow from a long workout. "How's it going, ladies?" she asked.

"Fine," chorused the pledges.

"Great. Try to finish up. We're going to have a meeting in a few minutes and I want to clear the foyer. Hey, KC," she said, smiling as she passed. "Those cubbies are looking mighty fine."

"Thanks," said KC, proud of the job she'd done.

"How'd you get stuck with that job?"

"I volunteered."

"You're kidding!"

"It's sort of fun cleaning something this grimy," said KC. "Like raking a yard covered with leaves, or washing a mud-caked car." What she didn't tell Diane was that she couldn't risk working on the posters. One drop of neon paint, one stroke of indelible marker, could ruin her clothes. Unlike her sorority sisters, she couldn't afford to just run out and replace a ruined blouse or skirt. Her parents were already struggling to pay her tuition, and at the moment, KC didn't have a part-time job.

"Anybody see the glue stick?"

"One more minute. We're nearly through."

"We've got tape over here. Will that help?"

"No, gotta have glue."

KC's hands burned every time she stuck them into the bucket; the cleaning solvent was much too strong for her sensitive skin. Her hands were red and raw. "Done," she said, wiping a rag around the last cubby. She stepped back to admire her work.

"Looks great, KC," called Courtney Conner as

she sailed gracefully down the front stairs. The ends of the long silk scarf she'd tossed around her neck floated out behind her. KC beamed at the compliment. She could still hardly believe that of all the pledges to choose from, Tri Beta's president had singled her out as a friend.

Courtney stood on the last step and clapped her hands a few times. "Attention, please, everyone." She waited for the pledges to quiet down. The sun streaming in from the window at the top of the stairs filtered through her blond hair. Courtney clapped her hands again. "I need you all in the living room for a quick meeting," she said.

"Can we leave our stuff here?" someone asked. "We're nearly done."

"Yes," said Courtney. "This won't take long."

KC joined the dash to the living room, flopping down with the others on the thick rug. "Oh, no," she said softly, looking at her shoes. The cleaning solvent had splashed on her patent leather pumps and eaten little, round holes through the finish. The shoes, by far her most comfortable pair, were ruined.

"That's a shame," said Marcia Tabbert next to her. "But I saw a pair just like those last week at Vogue Shoes. I'm sure they still have them."

"Thanks," said KC, trying to smile. There was

no way she could buy a new pair of shoes right now. She wouldn't have that kind of money until after she worked all summer. Being short of funds wasn't a problem that would even occur to someone like Marcia who received unlimited money from her parents.

"First," said Courtney, "I want to tell you how fabulous the house is beginning to look. Maybe we should have open house every week."

"Noooo."

"Booo."

"Hissss." Protests went up around the room.

Courtney held up her hands, laughing, quieting the group down.

"All right, all right," she said. "Anyway, the house really sparkles. That's the good news, but I'm afraid I have some bad news to go along with it. It seems that the city inspectors who came through here last week didn't like a few things they saw. We need to rewire the entire house to bring it up to the new safety codes. And we have to buy a new boiler as well as do roof repairs. Unfortunately, all these things cost a great deal of money. What it all comes down to, I'm afraid, is that we are going to have to raise our monthly dues."

KC felt the world drop out from under her.

Courtney kept talking but KC couldn't hear. *Raise dues. Raise dues,* KC repeated in her mind. She could barely afford the dues now! If it wasn't for a secret stash her Grandma Rose had sent to cover Greek expenses, she wouldn't be able to pledge Tri Beta at all. And KC had used part of that money to hire a tutor when her grades slipped.

Asking her parents for more money was totally out of the question. Not only were they straining to pay tuition, room, and board, but they absolutely hated the Greek system.

"Sororities are elitist and exclusive," they'd said. "They are hurtful to people who are not invited to join."

KC's parents were as prejudiced against the rich as other people were against the poor. But they would be shocked if KC ever said that to them. They thought of themselves as fair-minded, justice-for-all types.

The only solution was to find a part-time job. KC had never been afraid of hard work. Since coming to U. of S., she'd waited tables at the Beanery and worked as a dorm mail person. The trouble was, a job meant less time to study, less time to hang around Tri Beta, less time to be with Peter. KC's world, the same world that had looked so beautiful a couple of hours ago, began to cloud over.

After the meeting, she took her rags and bucket of dirty water into the kitchen to clean up. Courtney came in and grabbed a carrot out of the refrigerator.

"I am nearing the absolute limit of my energy," she said, slumping against the counter. "This week is doing me in. Sometimes I think how much easier my life would be if I weren't president."

"But you're so good at it," said KC. "No one else in Tri Beta could do the job you do."

Courtney smiled. "Thanks, KC, but sometimes it's hard to try and live my life and juggle the problems of all the other sisters." KC looked away. She wouldn't pile her money problems on Courtney. She finished cleaning the bucket and rags, and set them back in the corner. Courtney took another carrot out of the fridge and handed it to KC.

"Thanks," said KC, reaching for the carrot, trying not to sound as depressed as she felt.

Courtney gasped. "KC! Look at your hands! You come right upstairs with me this second." She grabbed KC's wrist and led her up to her room. "Sit," she said, making space on her bed among a jungle of stuffed animals. KC sat. Courtney opened her bottom desk drawer and started digging through a collection of tubes, bottles, and jars. "Here!" she said, triumphantly holding up a tube of salve. She unscrewed the cap and squirted a long coil of yellow ointment onto the backs of KC's hands. Slowly, gently, she rubbed the healing salve into KC's skin.

"Oh," said KC, "that feels so good."

"You should have asked for rubber gloves," said Courtney.

"I didn't want to bother anyone," said KC. "Like you said, everyone has things on their mind."

Something in KC's voice made Courtney look up. "KC, what's wrong?" KC shook her head, afraid if she talked she'd start crying.

"Something with Peter?" prodded Courtney. "Is our favorite photographer giving you a hard time?"

"No. Really, we're fine." How could KC tell Courtney she couldn't afford any more money for the sorority? There probably wasn't another girl in Tri Beta who gave money a second thought. "How's everything with you and Phoenix?" asked KC, determined to turn the conversation away from her.

"Good," said Courtney, "Although I really have to laugh. I mean, here I am, a junior, dating a freshman. And, as if that's not incredible enough, he loves hiking and camping and just about every other thing I hate. He's the only guy I've ever dated who doesn't fall all over himself to open doors for me, and pull out chairs. He reads pop poetry and loves rock and roll. And he'd just as soon rent a movie on a Saturday night as go out to a fine restaurant."

KC nodded. "Why do you and I date guys so different from ourselves? We should be going out with business majors, guys in suits and ties, guys with stock portfolios and IRA's."

"A-men," said Courtney, recapping the ointment tube and wiping the excess off her hands. "Sometimes," she said, sitting on the bed next to KC, "I think I must be crazy to date Phoenix. And other times, I think he's the best thing to come into my life. I guess fate brought us together."

"I think we make our own fate," said KC. "I believe we get what we work for."

"I used to feel that way," said Courtney. "Until I got that concussion and was put in the hospital where Phoenix just happened to be working as an orderly. I mean, in my entire life I never once needed to go to a hospital. I really feel that our relationship was meant to be."

Courtney scooted off the bed again and went to

her closet. She brought out a shoe box filled with gloves and took out a pair of white cotton ones. "Put these on," she said.

"Courtney, this gunk will ruin your gloves."

"That's a pledge order." Courtney helped KC pull on the gloves. "This will let the salve work into your skin. Besides, I hardly need white gloves for the places Phoenix takes me to. We go to pizza joints, movies, long walks in the foothills. I am about to get even, though."

"How?"

"I made him promise that during *Week at the U* he'd come with me to the international economics lecture and modern dance recital." She covered the glove box and put it back in the closet.

KC tried to picture fun-loving Phoenix being interested in an economics lecture. "Better make sure he drinks lots of coffee," said KC. "Or he'll fall asleep."

Courtney laughed. "Good idea." She sat down next to KC and took an emery board off the night stand, smoothing her already perfect nails. "Of course, he made me agree to go to Forest Hall's All Dorm Pizza Party." She made a sour face. "You know how I feel about pizza."

KC stared down at her hands. The salve was working its soothing magic under the white gloves. If only there was some magic potion she could spread to come up with money for the new sorority payments. She hated talking about money. How could someone like Courtney understand what it felt like to have to choose between buying a new lipstick or buying lunch? Still, if anyone could help her, it was Courtney.

"I . . . I've been thinking of getting a job," KC said, her face turning red. "My expenses are a little higher than I thought they would be."

"You are really a very special person," Courtney said.

"Me?" said KC. "Wha—"

"Yes, you. I wish I had twenty more pledges like you."

KC held up her gloves. "You want twenty girls with red hands and no money?"

Courtney smiled. "Look at the way you handle a problem. Instead of folding up and blowing away, instead of yelling and whining, you plant your feet and fight. When most people come up against a wall they turn around and go back. Not you. You look for another way around. One of the reasons you stand out from the rest of the pledges is that you are independent. Most of the other girls never had to rely on themselves."

KC felt the warm glow of friendship. How had

she ever thought Courtney would look down on her for having to work to pay for the things she wanted? "Thanks," she said. "That makes me feel a little better. And you're right, I don't mind working. The trouble is, I hate to take all that time away from the sorority and . . . well, other things, but I'll have to."

Courtney nodded. "Maybe one of the problems is the jobs you've had. Waiting tables and working as a dorm mail person pay a little money for a lot of time. What we need to find you is a job that pays a lot of money for a little time."

"Bank robbery," said KC.

"That might be a little bit risky, not to mention illegal." Courtney hummed to herself, thinking. Suddenly, she stopped, her face brightening. "That's it!" she said.

"What is?"

"Look, I know Phoenix is no business whiz, but he is always saying our best assets are our natural resources. And I think you're ignoring the one truly fabulous resource that's right in front of your face. In fact, it *is* your face!" Courtney jumped up and brought her hand mirror to KC, holding it in front of her.

KC looked into the mirror and made a fish face. "Very funny, KC. But I'm serious," Courtney continued. "Models make a small fortune. I bet you can earn more modeling in one runway session than in a week of waiting tables."

"Courtney, I don't know the first thing about modeling."

"That, my dear KC, is what sorority sisters are for. Come with me."

The two girls raced through the halls and up the steep steps to the attic. Courtney opened the door to a back room filled with filing cabinets. She pulled the chain to the overhead light.

"What's all this?" asked KC.

"We have here," said Courtney, "every paper ever written by a Tri Beta."

"You're kidding."

"Those tall, green, filing cabinets are test papers, everything from advertising to zoology. Some teachers actually give the exact same test over and over again. We have their names on file if you ever need an easy 'A,' but here," she pulled open a beige file cabinet drawer marked J, "are journalism papers. I remember Regina Charles did a report on modeling. Yes, here it is."

The two girls skimmed through the paper which listed two local agencies that handled runway models, TV commercial models, foot models, and hand models."

"This is perfect!" said KC, wiggling her white-gloved fingers. "Think I'll make my fortune with my hands?"

"Only if they're shooting a horror movie."

They laughed all the way back downstairs. KC took the folder, feeling like Courtney had just thrown her a lifeline. She'd call the agencies as soon as she got home and make appointments. *Someone is bound to need me to model something,* she thought.

Five

"Hi. My name is Kimberly Dayton."

"Yes?"

"I'm your physics lab partner."

"And?"

"And you were supposed to call me so we could meet to plan our experiment."

"Oh. Well, I'm very busy."

Kimberly replayed in her mind the conversation she'd had with Derek Weldon, the lab partner whose name she had picked out of a box. She couldn't believe he'd been so rude. And now that she was meeting him at eleven o'clock on Saturday morning, because that was the only time *he* had free, he was late.

"So where are you?" Kimberly drummed her fingers on one of the tables of the empty physics lab classroom.

"Whoever you are, *wherever* you are, Derek Weldon, you'd better get your sorry self into this room in the next five minutes or I'm leaving." Her voice echoed off the empty desks and unoccupied stools. Silence.

Kimberly sighed and looked at the scratchy handwriting covering the long chalk board. She didn't recognize the math, but knew it must be from theoretical physics or some other advanced class. She wondered if her studies in physics would take her that far. Would she ever be clever enough to understand all these formulas? Did she even want to?

"Yes," she said. "Yes, yes, and yes."

The big clock over the board ticked away. Five minutes. Six. Seven. Kimberly took out the library books she'd found with physics experiments. There were some fairly complex ones to demonstrate action and reaction. Many were out of the question because the supplies would cost a fortune. Kimberly had narrowed her choice to three that she thought would work well. She'd ask

Derek Weldon what he thought—if he ever showed up.

She walked over to the board. Balancing one leg sideways against the chalk ledge, she began stretching slowly. It was better to use the time limbering up than doing nothing at all. After a few stretches, she turned to the classroom and began slow ballet leaps up and down the rows. Ten more minutes passed. It wasn't fair that she had to conduct a difficult experiment with a nonexistent lab partner in the middle of rehearsals!

Finally, she stuffed her books back in her bag. "Well, Derek Weldon, if you're not concerned about this project, then neither am I."

Suddenly the door banged open and a tall mass of energy draped in black pleated pants and a blue shirt strode forward. Kimberly stared. His skin, the same color as her Uncle Nathaniel's, was what her grandmother called "coffee with two creams." And his brown eyes, even behind their wire-rimmed glasses, were big enough to fall into.

"You're late," was all she could think to say.

Derek stopped, staring at her. He shrugged his shoulders and sauntered to the table. "It's not my fault I need twenty-eight hours in the day to do everything I want to do." He plunked his bookbag down on the table.

"Well," said Kimberly, trying to ignore the strange flutter in her stomach, "it certainly isn't my fault, either. You're not the only one around here with things to do."

"I'll match my day against yours anytime," he said, sliding onto a stool. He took off his glasses and held them up to the light. Pulling a handkerchief out of his pocket, he huffed on a lens and began cleaning it. "I'm very involved in this *Week at the U.*" He huffed on the other lens and cleaned it, too. Then he glanced up at Kimberly. "I am single-handedly responsible for two major events and—"

Kimberly folded her arms tight across her chest, trying to keep her anger down. "Well," she said, "since your time is so *very* precious, perhaps we should get started."

"You know, it wouldn't kill you," he said, wrapping the wire eyeglass hooks back around his ears, "to be just a little sympathetic."

"About what? You don't come to class. You don't call me when you know perfectly well Prof. Jobst said you were supposed to. You keep me waiting fifteen minutes in this lab until you're good and ready to show up, and—"

"Hey, calm down. This is only one experiment. It's no big deal."

"And you're making me late for my rehearsal," Kimberly said, finishing the sentence he'd interrupted. "Of course, my dance performance isn't *nearly* as important as anything going on in your life. Except," she said slapping her hand on the counter, and making Derek jump, "it's something I've been training for my whole life. Except," she slapped the counter again, "I need all the time I can get to work on it. So don't you go telling me to be calm, Mr. I-have-so-much-to-do. And don't you be deciding what is or is not a big deal in my life."

Derek's jaw moved back and forth as he clenched his teeth. His nostrils flared. He looked like he was ready to explode.

"Then maybe we'd better get started," he said, trying to control his anger.

"Good." Kimberly opened a book. "I brought some library books on—"

"Here." He reached into his pocket and pulled out two large balloons. "Blow one up."

"I don't have time for games."

"Neither do I." He blew up one balloon until it was a huge, round ball. Climbing up on one of the lab tables, he held the balloon over his head.

"You are a crazy person," said Kimberly.

"That's what they say about all great scientists."

His smile caught her off guard and she smiled back before remembering how angry she was at him. "Now, this experiment is supposed to be about action-reaction, right?"

"Right."

"Something cannot be pushed, unless something else is pushing."

"That's what the law says."

"And something can't push unless there is something *to* push. Right?"

Kimberly nodded. He might be late and he might be arrogant, but Derek was also bright.

"Okay. We have a balloon. That's one thing. Then we have the air inside. That's another thing. Now, how do we show one pushing against the other and the other pushing back?" He let the balloon go and it zoomed around the room, diving and climbing, making crazy circles and waves, until it ran out of air and dropped to the floor.

"The air pushing against the balloon, the balloon pushing against the air inside, propels the balloon forward," Derek went on. "Action-reaction." He climbed down from the table. "Well? What do you think?"

Kimberly was speechless. She couldn't believe she'd spent so many hours at the library, weeding through advanced physics books only to end up with an experiment that any second grader could do. "That's your entire experiment?"

"I have enough balloons for everyone in class," Derek answered. "This experiment fulfills Prof. Jobst's requirements and, I think, it'll be fun. So I guess now we're set." He smiled, grabbed his things, and walked out of the room, leaving a stunned Kimberly to wonder whether she should laugh or cry or scream. *Maybe,* she thought, *I should do all three.*

Faith finished twisting the elastic band around the bottom of her braid, then tightened her fanny pack over her jeans skirt.

"Where are you going?" Liza asked, as she finished applying a second coat of bright, orange polish to her toenails.

"I promised to watch Kimberly rehearse," said Faith, the words out before she could stop them.

"Hey, great! I'll go, too."

"Oh, no. That is, she's not—"

Too late. Liza threw on a sweater, pulled socks and shoes right over her wet nails, smeared bright, red lipstick on her lips, and sprayed lilac cologne all over her red hair.

"Never hurts to pick up a few dance moves," she said, twirling comically.

"You must not say one single word," Faith said, laying down the law on the way to the dance studio. She couldn't let her raucous roommate make Kimberly nervous. "Kimberly is going to work on her dance and we are going to watch. That's all. We are going to be absolutely invisible. If you do one single thing to distract her, you'll have to leave."

"Sure thing," said Liza, putting a third piece of bubble gum into her mouth. She blew a huge bubble at three cute boys walking toward them. They laughed as it popped at the exact moment they passed. "I know how to fade into the background."

Faith rolled her eyes, and the two of them walked on in silence until they reached the door of the dance studio Kimberly was supposed to be rehearsing in. Three walls of the large room were mirrored. Barres were mounted on the glass and dancers worked out at the thick, waist-high poles, stretching, warming up, working on body angles and hand-and-foot movements. Their clothes were as varied as their body shapes: leotards with and without feet, cut-off sweats, loose tops, chiffon scarves tied at waists and necks.

"I don't see Kimberly," said Faith. Three girls in ballet shoes ran up, sliding their shoes into the rosin box near the door. Two couples working on a jazz routine pushed past them.

Liza found a chair right next to the door and plopped down.

"Oh no," Faith warned. "We've got to get out of the way. Let's go back there."

"Back where?"

"Over in the corner," Faith said, pointing to where coats and dance bags were piled. "We can stay near the piano where all the extra ballet barres are stored."

"All the way back there!" Liza complained. "We'll never see anything."

What Liza really meant was that no one would see her, which was exactly what Faith intended. Kimberly was nervous enough without Liza trying to take center stage—again. They settled into the corner, even though Liza kept stretching her feet toward the dance floor.

Just then Kimberly raced in and tossed her coat and packs into the pile. Faith thought she looked upset.

"Hi," said Faith, waving.

Kimberly's eyes widened in surprise. She smiled. "Hi! You made it."

"Me, too!" said Liza, jumping up.

Faith shrugged at Kimberly and Kimberly nodded as if to say "I understand. It's hard to lose a shadow."

"Sorry I'm late," said Kimberly. "It's my lab partner's fault."

"Kimberly," called a petite woman from across the room. "Let's get to work."

"That's Ms. Zarkin, my advisor and modern dance teacher," explained Kimberly. "She's the one who chose me to perform. I'd better go."

Faith watched Kimberly limber up, and begin to work with her teacher. Something was definitely wrong. When Kimberly was just kidding around in the dorm, her dancing was fluid and graceful. Today her body seemed tight.

"Kimberly, Kimberly," called Ms. Zarkin from across the room. "Lighter, easier, relax, relax. Da-dum deedle-dee." The teacher swayed to the music, lifting her hands up and up, trying to lighten Kimberly's steps.

"My feet feel like concrete blocks," said Kimberly. "I just can't get into the dance today."

"Don't worry so much about getting each step exactly right," said Ms. Zarkin, coming over to dance next to Kimberly. The teacher seemed to float on air. "Think about the meaning of the piece, the flow of the music. It's like the great musicians. Anyone can play all the notes exactly right, but only the great ones—the Rubensteins, the Van Clyburns—go beyond the notes into the heart of the music. Feel it. Da-dum, deedle-dee. That's better. Lighter. Yes, yes. More like that. Yes. Good."

Faith watched every move, trying to think of something that would help her friend get through the night of the performance.

"She'll never get it," whispered Liza, who'd been making comments on all the dancers.

"Shhhh," said Faith, for the umpteenth time. Did all directors have would-be stars hanging on them all the time? Liza began swaying to the music, getting up to dance in the corner. Faith gave up. Was there ever a more impossible person?

Suddenly the studio doors swung open, sending the tacked up Keep Out—Rehearsal sign flying across the room. Faith gasped. Kimberly froze. Liza squealed. Christopher Hammond in all his handsome, snobbish glory, breezed into the rehearsal room, trailed by a camera crew from the local TV station where he was an intern.

"Hello," he said, flashing his phony smile at the startled dancers.

Faith thought that Christopher's sport jacket and tie looked ridiculously out of place in the work-out setting. But if he felt out of place, he didn't show it. Snake-cool as ever, he said, "I'm here to tape a TV segment. Who's in charge?"

Ms. Zarkin rushed over to talk to him.

In Faith's entire life, there had been only two or three people who had ever made her really angry. Christopher Hammond was right at the head of that list. They had met early in the first semester when Faith assisted him in a student production he was directing. Her ideas had made his production a hit, and soon the two of them were an item. At least, until Faith discovered he was two-timing her. On top of that deceit, Christopher had humiliated Lauren for a fraternity prank, he'd stood by while an innocent boy was dangerously hazed during fraternity rush, and he'd helped elderly citizens only when he was sure TV cameras were recording his good deed. The long list of grievances Faith had against him went on and on.

"What's he doing here?" asked Kimberly, coming to wait with Faith. She blotted sweat from her forehead with a small towel.

"I don't know."

"I recognize him!" cried Liza. "He's somebody."

"He's nobody," Faith muttered. "I ought to know."

Faith strained to hear what Christopher was saying to Ms. Zarkin. She picked up bits and pieces. ". . . promotional bit . . . lead shots of rehearsal . . . show behind the show . . ." Ms. Zarkin backed away, obviously agreeing to let the crew set up according to Christopher's directions.

"Over here," he said to the camera crew. "Get the barre in the background and maybe that old grand piano."

"All right, Kimberly, Florence, Martha." The teacher waved a few students back onto the floor. "Let's go through our usual warm-ups."

"Now?" asked Kimberly, her voice quavering.

"Yes. Hurry, please."

Ms. Zarkin led the dancers in some easy warm-ups for the cameras. Faith held her breath as Kimberly, painfully self-conscious, tried to move around the floor. She looked more like a puppet jerking on a string than the strong, graceful dancer Faith knew she was. How could Christopher do this? Furious, she stepped out from behind the piano, and grabbed Christopher's arm.

"Faith!" Surprised, he let her pull him out into the deserted hall.

Faith closed the door, muffling Ms. Zarkin's voice calling out warm-up positions and movements. "How could you do that?" Faith tried to yell in a whisper.

"Well, well, well, the famous freshman director." Christopher closed his eyes halfway in his old, sexy look.

Faith didn't fall for it. "How can you come crashing into a rehearsal?" she asked. "Didn't you see the Do Not Disturb sign on the door?"

"Got a great shot of it," he said. "We'll use it in our lead-in."

"I don't believe you. You should know better than to barge in on people. How would you like me pushing into your TV studio during a shoot?" He reached out and lifted a strand of hair off her neck. She felt goose bumps rise on her arms.

"I'm sorry you're so upset, Faith, but I have a job to do. I'm supposed to scout footage of the *Week at the U* preparations. Photographing science department experiments doesn't make for riveting TV. A dance rehearsal is much more visually exciting. As a director, you should be able to appreciate that. And I didn't barge in," he said, with an edge to his voice. "I received permission from the head of the dance department."

Every bit of rage Faith had ever felt for Christopher rose up inside of her. She was about to say something to put him in his place when she heard the door open behind her. She turned away, forcing herself to cool down. It would be horrible of

her to start a public fight right in the middle of
Kimberly's rehearsal. Poor Kimberly was so keyed
up already that one more disruption might very
well send her out of the room crying. No matter
how angry Faith was with Christopher, she would
control herself until a more appropriate time.

"You're not *the* Christopher Hammond are
you?" boomed the foghorn voice behind her.
Faith stared open-mouthed as Liza pushed past
her. Liza grabbed Christopher's hand, pumping it
vigorously up and down. "I *love* those human in-
terest pieces you do. How on earth do you find all
those fascinating things going on on campus?"

Faith shook her head. If ever there were two
people who deserved each other, two people who
thought they were better than everyone and anyone else around, it was Liza Ruff and Christopher
Hammond.

"I'm glad to know you're a fan," Christopher
said, flashing his practiced smile at Liza. "Now if
you'll excuse me, I'd better get back in there. I
want to be sure my crew gets the shots I want."

His crew. Faith rolled her eyes for the second
time that day. *Was there no end to his ego?*

"Wait," Liza pulled out a pen and a scrap of
paper, "I have some great ideas for your show.

Why don't you give me your home phone number and I'll call you tonight."

"Okay," said Christopher, jotting down his number. "I have a machine on so you can leave a message if I'm not in."

Liza tucked the number into her purse, looking very much like the cat who ate the canary. Christopher went back into the rehearsal hall to finish the shoot. Faith stood at the door, unable to go back in. How could she watch Kimberly suffer in front of the camera? Liza pushed the door open and watched Kimberly dance. Faith couldn't help looking over her shoulder.

"Kimberly's going to have a kitten when she sees herself on television," said Liza. "She looks more like the Tin Man of Oz than a modern dance major.

It was true. Kimberly was practically frozen in front of the camera.

"Can we see part of a dance to music?" asked Christopher, moving the cameras around.

"Of course," said Ms. Zarkin. "Kimberly?" she said, walking to the tape player, hitting the button to begin "The Sorcerer's Apprentice."

Faith watched as Kimberly straightened her long back, lifted her proud chin and changed from caterpillar to butterfly. As if the music was flowing through her body, her arms softened, her legs took on a new lightness. *Yes,* thought Faith. *The music is mightier than the TV camera. Come on, Kimberly, you can do it!* Light, powerful, dramatic, Kimberly forgot her surroundings. This was the real Kimberly—the beautiful dancer who could enter the rhythm of the music and bend it, shape it, dance it.

One of the camerawomen, backing up to get a long shot, tripped over her cable and crashed to the floor. The sound broke Kimberly out of her concentration and once again she became aware of the cameras and people watching her.

Faith pushed past Liza and hurried back into the rehearsal room, pulling a chair right up front where Kimberly could see her. She smiled at her friend in encouragement.

Kimberly flashed a weak smile in return, struggling to get back on step. At least she hadn't given up. *And that,* thought Faith, *is a start in the right direction.*

Six

•••••••••••••

"*And will you be mine forever and ever?*" *Josh's blazing eyes burned through Winnie, igniting her heart, setting her deepest passion on fire.*

"*Oh, yes, Josh, I will!*" *She leaned into him as he wrapped her in his strong arms and* . . .

"Winnie? Winnie? Yoooo-hoooooo, earth-to-Winnie."

Winnie's eyes snapped back into focus. Josh disappeared. Instead Faith, Kimberly, and KC sat at the dining commons breakfast table, staring at her. She smiled at them blankly.

"Winnie, if you're back with the living, could you please pass the syrup?" KC asked.

"Oh, sure." Winnie reached down the long, wooden table, holding back her floppy kimono sleeve as she rescued the syrup pitcher from a group of football players. "Sorry," she said, handing the syrup to KC.

"I don't know where your thoughts were on this Tuesday morning," said Faith, "but they sure seemed far away."

I was thinking about Josh, Winnie thought to herself. *I was dreaming about meeting him in his room this morning.* She tilted back on her chair and pushed her bracelets up on her arms. She was dying to jump up on the table and scream Josh and Winnie are in love! But she forced herself to wait. This time she wasn't going to rush things.

"Do you think Winnie might have something besides breakfast on her mind this morning?" asked Kimberly, tucking an orange into her dance bag.

"Or someone," said KC.

"Why ever would you say that?" asked Faith, winking. "Just because she's cut her pancakes into a heart shape, carved in the initials WG and JG, and decorated the edges with powdered sugar?"

Winnie looked down at her plate. When had she

done that? "I'm not really hungry," she said, pulling on her dinosaur earring. Winnie set her juice next to her heart-shaped pancake. She couldn't eat, not with her stomach tied up in nervous knots just thinking about the feel of Josh's arms around her, and the warmth of his kiss.

"Well," said Kimberly, tugging up her leg warmers, "you can be sure I'm never going to fall in love. Not if it means losing my appetite for blueberry pancakes."

"Oh, I don't know," said Faith, a sudden smile lighting up her face. "Looks to me like love makes some people downright hungry." She wiggled her eyebrows at someone behind Winnie.

They all turned. Josh was coming through the end of the food line, his tray piled high with pancakes, cereal, milk, juice, and fruit. Winnie's heart hammered in her chest. The stubble of beard he'd had the last time she saw him was shaved. His long, dark hair was shampooed and combed. He had on a fresh T-shirt under his leather jacket, and he wore clean, faded jeans.

"I thought you said Josh wasn't a breakfast person," said Kimberly.

"He . . . he's not," said Winnie.

"Guess he couldn't wait for you to come to

him," said KC. "He had to come see you. Ahh-hhh, love."

"You guys," said Winnie, crumpling her napkin and throwing it at KC. What was he doing here so early? She wasn't ready. She'd wanted to respike her hair and change into funkier clothes before she saw him.

"I don't know what you're sitting around with us for," said KC, winking at the others. "If I had a hunk like that waiting for me, I'd be up and gone by now."

"Ditto," said Faith.

"Double ditto," said Kimberly.

Winnie made a face at her friends and stood up. "Well, I hate to eat and run," she said, picking up her tray.

"We expect to hear every delicious detail later on," said Kimberly.

Winnie smiled. *This is it,* she thought, making her way to Josh. *Where is it written that we can't begin our relationship right here, right now. I'll tell him how I feel. So what if 200 people overhear?*

"Hi," said Josh. "I remember you."

"You look familiar, too," said Winnie.

They stood, tray to tray, as still as two rocks. A stream of students flowed around them. "I think we'd better sit down," said Josh.

"Good idea." They found two empty chairs against a wall and sat across from each other, their knees accidentally touching under the table. Winnie could hardly breathe. Josh attacked the pile of pancakes.

Winnie watched, fascinated. She couldn't eat a bite when she was this nervous, but it looked as if Josh was just the opposite. He was also just the opposite of Travis Bennett, Winnie's big Paris romance in the summer months between high school and college. Travis, someone who took what he wanted when he wanted it, had shown up at U. of S. to convince Winnie to go away with him, but by that time, Winnie had met Josh. Josh was more gentle, more caring, more giving than Travis could ever be. She had finally sent Travis packing. Now, watching Josh, feeling closer than ever to him, Winnie knew she'd made the right choice.

"I didn't expect to see you here," Winnie rambled in motor-mouth speed. "I mean, I expected to see you this morning, just later this morning, back in your room, not now in the dining commons over pancakes. I know how you hate getting up early. Actually, I hate getting up early, too. Anytime before ten is the middle of the night to me." She giggled. "I'm doing it again. My mouth is on overload. Shut me up."

Josh laughed. "I stayed up so many hours to finish my project that my body doesn't know what time it is," he said. "I just know I'm here. You're here. And that puts me on overload, too."

"We're here," Winnie beamed. "Pancakes are here. The rest of the dorms are here."

Josh winked and touched his earring. "Great place for a romantic reunion."

Winnie threw a blueberry at him. "Listen, after the amount of time that we've had to spend apart, my psych lab would be a good enough place to meet you."

Josh winced. "With all those caged monkeys?"

"And the rats," Winnie remembered. "Ugh. Never mind. I take it back."

Josh stopped eating and looked at her with the warmest smile. "God, I've missed you, Win. Let's not ever fight again. Let's not ever be apart again."

"It's a deal."

They gazed at each other, then sat for a while eating and smiling, eating and smiling.

"I can't believe we're actually sitting here like this," said Winnie.

"It *has* been a long time coming," said Josh. Turning his palms up, he wiggled his fingers until

Winnie slid her hands into his. Her heart raced as he closed his fingers over hers. "I can't remember why we waited so long to get together."

"Doesn't matter, now." Winnie stroked her thumbs over his skin, feeling the current running through her, into him, and back again.

"I've wanted to talk to you," he said. "So many times I've stopped outside your door, trying to get up the nerve to knock—"

"Oh, me too! When that whole mix-up happened with Travis—"

"I was stupid. I don't know why I wouldn't believe you'd broken up with him. It was just that I was so jealous. I couldn't bear to see a guy you'd loved come back into your life. It drove me crazy.

"I know. And I acted stupidly, too. At first I didn't want to hurt Travis's feelings by telling him to leave, but I ended up hurting you instead. I was terrified I'd lost you forever. So that night when you called the Hotline—"

Josh jerked back as if Winnie had jolted him with a thousand volts.

Winnie bit her lip. She hadn't meant to blurt out the last sentence. "I mean . . . I didn't want. . . . Oh, Josh."

"That was *you* on the Crisis Hotline?" he asked in disbelief. "I thought it was your voice, but when you didn't identify yourself I figured it must be someone who sounded like you."

"I couldn't tell you who I was," said Winnie.

"Why not?"

"Josh, you've got to understand. When I volunteered at the Hotline, I took an oath. I'm not allowed to give callers my name."

"You could have given my call to another volunteer," Josh pointed out. "Heck, I didn't even know you were working there." The warmth in his eyes had turned icy. She felt him slipping away from her. When he spoke again, she could hear his anger and hurt. "Why did you let me go on and on like that?"

"Your call caught me off guard," explained Winnie. "It was my first night on the Hotline, and by the time I realized I should do something, it was too late to stop you."

"I poured my heart out to you like an idiot."

"You didn't sound like an idiot to me," she said, trying to calm Josh down. Winnie knew he had reason to be upset, but he wasn't trying to understand.

Josh stood up. "You say you had responsibilities to the Hotline. But what about me? Didn't I mean anything to you? Didn't you feel any responsibility to me?" He picked up his tray, knocking over his chair as he stepped back. Heads turned. "Maybe you should rethink your priorities."

He walked toward the conveyor belt. Winnie grabbed her tray and followed.

"Josh, wait!" He didn't slow down. Winnie pushed through the crowds, trying to keep up with him. People turned.

Josh was already scraping his tray when she reached the conveyor. She talked as fast as she could, trying to keep him from walking away again. "I know how embarrassed you must feel—"

"Don't tell me what I'm feeling!" Josh shouted as he whirled around to face her. "You don't know what I'm feeling."

"Don't you understand, I was just trying to do one thing right. I'm always lousing everything up. I thought, this time, I'd really try to follow the rules."

"You picked a fine time to start." Josh turned his back on her and strode toward the dining commons exit.

"Josh, please!"

He stopped, one hand on the exit door. She pushed through the pancake line, struggling to catch up with him. "I didn't mean to hurt you. You've got to trust me."

Winnie felt everyone staring at them but she

didn't care. All that mattered was that Josh didn't walk through the door and leave her. This was supposed to be a new beginning, not the final curtain.

"I like who's talking about trust." He moved aside to let a group walk out.

"What's that supposed to mean?"

"How am I supposed to trust someone who runs around behind my back with an old boyfriend?"

"I told you that's over," she said. "Travis means nothing to me and you know it. What do you want me to do? Tattoo your name across my forehead?"

"I don't want you to do anything," said Josh, moving back to the door.

"You can't leave me like this!"

"You should have told me it was you on the Hotline. I can't just let that go. I've got to have some time to think this over."

"What about me? What about us?"

"I don't know, Winnie. But if you and I are ever going to have any kind of relationship, it can't be based on deception."

He slammed his hand against the swinging door and stormed out of the dining hall, out of the building, out of her life.

Winnie swallowed back the tears. *Nice going, Winnie,* she thought. *You just created another big mess.*

She walked out of the building and stared off at the mountains. Anger pushed in on her sorrow. What was she feeling so sorry about? This wasn't all her fault. Josh Gaffey had done a bang-up job on her feelings, too. He'd taken her heart and smashed it into a thousand little pieces.

Seven

P hoenix Cates stood next to Courtney and her friends in the crowded lobby of Ridgefield Hall, as they waited for the auditorium doors to open. Students, teachers, parents, local politicians, and Springfield alumni mingled in clusters around a large, crystal punch bowl. Phoenix felt like he was drowning in a sea of well-dressed humanity.

"Is this whole week going to be like this?" he asked.

Courtney smiled and slipped her arm through his. "Opening night of *Week at the U* is always special," she explained. "When I was a freshman, a lot of women came to this kick-off party dressed in long gowns. Men wore tuxedos."

It was a good thing Courtney had casually suggested Phoenix might want to dress up for this lecture. If she hadn't, he would have picked her up in his usual green scrub shirt, jeans, and beaded cowboy belt.

"Why do they make such a big deal over the *Week at the U?*" he asked.

"Economics," said Maddox Wright, one of Courtney's friends. "College enrollment is down all over the country. That means there's less scholarship money and tuition is up. Schools have to beat those old tom-toms loud and clear to drum up new recruits and donations."

"Right," said Phoenix.

He shifted from foot to foot, trying to take his mind off the way his "dress" shoes pinched his feet. The stiff shirt collar and tie strangling his neck weren't any more comfortable. He wondered how Maddox, who was wearing a bow tie, starched collar, and tweed sports jacket with patches at the elbows could dress like that every day.

"Well, I say it's high time the United States returned to an isolationist policy toward . . ." one of Courtney's friends was saying.

"That's absurd," said another.

"The problem with that," Courtney interjected gently, "is—"

Every time Phoenix thought he understood what they were talking about, they took off in another direction. Of all the *interesting* things he and Courtney could have gone to on opening night of *The Week at the U*—like the fencing demonstration, or a screening of the original Japanese film *The Seven Samurai,* or a rock concert performed by Russian exchange students—why had Courtney picked the international economics lecture?

"Stand back please, we'd like to get some cameras in here." Local TV reporters moved in with camera crews.

"We're going to find seats," said Maddox. "See you later."

"We'd better get out of the way, too," said Phoenix, leading Courtney to a quieter spot, away from where the president of the university was about to give an interview. "Can I get you some more punch?" he asked.

"Thanks, no. I'm fine. We'll go in soon."

Person after person came up to say hello to Courtney. Phoenix stepped aside, watching. She looked more beautiful than usual. Her teal angora cardigan highlighted the intense blue of her eyes, and her suede dress was as soft as her skin. Her blond hair was pulled up in a chic twist. Phoenix wanted to remove all the pins and let her hair fall free to her shoulders. Instead, he put his arm around Courtney's waist. "It's not too late to go see *The Seven Samurai*," he said.

She slid her hand under his tie, straightening it. "Phoenix Cates, you promised that I could pick tonight's program."

He held up his hands in surrender. "Just a suggestion."

The lobby lights flashed the five-minute warning. "We'd better go in," she said.

They had to walk around the TV crews still taping interviews. "Let's see if we can sneak behind the president," said Phoenix. "Maybe we can wave at the cameras while he talks. I'll bet we can get ourselves on the evening news."

Courtney laughed. "Behave," she said.

Phoenix frowned and followed her into the auditorium, down the red-carpeted aisle to seats in the fifth row, center.

"I usually sit last row, last balcony," he said, settling in next to her in the plush seats, their elbows touching on the armrest.

Someone in the row behind them touched Courtney's shoulder. "Hi," said KC. "I looked for you in the lobby but it was such a madhouse." She wore her Tri Beta pledge pin on her blazer jacket.

"I thought Peter was coming with you," said Courtney.

"He did," said KC. "Sort of. There he is." She pointed to a guy in an old football shirt and jeans setting a large camera bag on the edge of the stage. "Peter wanted to photograph the kick-off party and this lecture for the school paper."

Phoenix watched Peter take light readings up on stage with a hand-held meter. "He's got the right idea," he said. "Photographers don't have to wear ties and suit jackets. And he can walk out after the first five minutes. I wonder if he could use an assistant," Phoenix said, starting to stand up.

Courtney pulled him back down, growling softly. "Don't you dare," she said. KC laughed.

The house lights dimmed. Three men from the faculty and one woman from an out-of-state university walked up onto the stage. The audience applauded politely as they took their seats at a long table. "Ladies and gentlemen," began the introductory speaker, "on behalf of University of Springfield, I want to welcome you to opening night of *Week at the U*. It is my honor this evening, to introduce our distinguished panel. On my left, we have the eminent Professor Mattison from—"

He droned on and on, introducing each speaker, giving a little history. Then the woman, Professor Mattison, spoke next.

Phoenix hated her voice. It sounded like a single note played on a bad trumpet, with no ups and downs, no quality. Phoenix didn't know how students could stay awake in her classes.

"She's a brilliant professor," whispered Courtney. "She's advised two presidents."

"Advised them to do what?"

"Shhhh," said a woman sitting in front of them.

"Sorry," said Courtney.

Phoenix tried, but he couldn't follow what the woman was saying. Instead, he took Courtney's hand. Her skin was so pale next to his, her fingers so delicate. They certainly weren't the hands of someone who back-packed on weekend trips and foraged in the woods for food like he did. But thinking about Courtney and the time they'd spent together helped him keep awake until the torture finally ended. He jumped up as soon as the house lights came on, bending his knees a few times to get them working.

"Wasn't that fabulous?" asked KC.

"Yes. Mattison really makes complex issues easy to understand."

Phoenix stared at them. He certainly hadn't enjoyed a word.

Out in the lobby, the string quartet had been replaced by a banjo, guitar, and mandolin group playing bluegrass. Phoenix stood between KC and Courtney, smiling as they discussed the lecture. *This is more like it,* he thought. Not only was the music more to his liking, but he enjoyed standing with the two most beautiful women in the place. It almost made up for having to sit through an hour-and-a-half-long discussion on economics. Peter came up, putting away his cameras, marking the rolls of film in his bag.

"What'd you think of the lecture?" asked Phoenix.

Peter shrugged. "I was so busy working that I didn't really pay attention." He slipped his arm around KC. "You're going to have to explain it all to me," he said.

"Not tonight," said KC. "I have to get my beauty sleep before my appointment tomorrow."

"KC's interviewing with a modeling agency in the morning," explained Courtney.

"Ten o'clock." KC's face glowed with excitement.

"KC," said Courtney, "you have to promise to call me right after the interview. I'm dying to find out what happens. Modeling's always seemed so exotic."

"I will," said KC. "See you tomorrow." She grabbed Peter's hand and pulled him through the crowd.

Phoenix wanted to leave, too, but other students walked up to them, everyone excited about the lecture. The group closed in around Courtney.

"I'm thinking of going to grad school where Mattison teaches," said a bearded guy next to Phoenix.

"I'm interviewing with several Wall Street firms for a summer internship," another gushed.

"What did you think of the lecture?" Courtney asked, trying to draw Phoenix into their conversation.

"Well," said Phoenix, pulling off his tie and unbuttoning his jacket, "I think it would have been better if they had served popcorn."

He smiled, enjoying his joke. No one smiled back.

A grad student nodded at Phoenix. "Your little brother," he said to Courtney, "has quite the sense of humor."

"Now the isolationist policy—" someone began.

Phoenix didn't listen. He stood frozen to the spot. Why didn't Courtney say something? Wasn't it up to her to set everyone straight? Wasn't it up to her to say "This is not my little brother. This is my boyfriend." She didn't.

Phoenix excused himself and went to the men's room, staying there long enough to give the group time to break up and go home. He found Courtney waiting for him near the door, and they walked out into the night in silence.

"Mmmmm," she said, breathing deeply, "what a lovely night."

Phoenix didn't take her hand. Instead, he shoved his hands deep into his pockets and walked silently beside her. *It was up to her to make the first move. Courtney should apologize. I'm the one who was insulted.*

They walked past the empty buildings, Courtney's high heels clicking on the concrete path. Phoenix hated the silence. He hated not hearing her voice, or her laughter.

What am I so angry about, anyway? Courtney wasn't the one who insulted me. Suddenly he had an idea. "You are," he said, "the slowest runner in the history of the university."

"What?" From the surprise on her face, he knew that whatever she was expecting him to say, that sure wasn't it.

"Yup. Word is out on you, Conners. I'll bet if I

raced you to the sculpture garden, you wouldn't get there until noon tomorrow."

"Now?" she asked.

"Now," he said. He saw the glint in her eye as she slowly bent down and took off her high heels.

"You happen to be looking at a former captain of the Worthington School for Girls rugby team," she said, suddenly sprinting off toward the sculpture garden. Caught off guard, Phoenix took off after her. *"Champion* rugby team," she called over her shoulder. "And soccer. And crew."

They raced through the quad and out toward the garden that overflowed with a mix of classical statues and abstract art forms. Phoenix rounded a corner too fast, his shoes skidding out from under him, pitching him down on the ground. Courtney laughed, running harder than ever as he struggled to get up.

"If anyone is out of shape around here," she yelled, "it is a certain mountain man."

"Out of shape?" he called, racing after her. "I'll show you who's out of shape." He caught her as she touched the statue at the entrance to the sculpture garden.

"I win! I win!" she yelled, squealing as Phoenix swept her up in his arms and whirled her around in circles.

"You cheated," he said, gasping for breath, carrying her to The Monster, a pretzel-shaped piece of sculpture in the center of the garden. Setting her down, he bent over her, lifting her face to his, kissing her long and hard on the mouth.

"Now," he said, softly, "is that a little brother kiss?"

"Don't even think about that," said Courtney. "That guy is a dolt. He didn't mean anything by it. Just forget it."

"Forget what?" asked Phoenix, as he reached for her and they kissed again.

Eight

......•......

"Y ou look like Peter Pan," said Faith.

"Think so?" said Kimberly, frowning. She'd thrown a loose, green top over her black Flexitard and tights and belted it low on her hips. "I wanted to look like a pirate," she said. "In honor of the fencing exhibition."

"I think you look exactly like a pirate," said Winnie.

"I'm lucky I have *any* clothes on," said Faith, looking down at her denim skirt. "I was so busy worrying about Liza tagging along with us tonight, that I ducked out when she started organizing her tapes of Broadway musicals. It wasn't until

I got outside that I remembered my jacket. I had to sneak back in and grab it without her seeing me."

"What do you care?" asked Winnie. She shook her spiky hair. "So what if you hurt Liza's feelings? Why should you have to invite her along every single minute?"

"Because," said Kimberly, draping her arms over Faith and Winnie's shoulders as they walked across campus toward the gym, "our buddy Faith here is a nice person."

"I am not," said Faith.

"Kimberly's right," said Winnie. "You *are* a real softy. Anyone else would have strangled Liza Ruff seven times over by now."

"Eight," agreed Kimberly.

"Nine," said Faith. "She's just so embarrassing, the way she pushes herself into things. Ever since Christopher and his camera crew barged into Kimberly's dance rehearsal, Liza has been calling him every day." She sighed, blowing out her cheeks. "Even in acting class, where we're *supposed* to be showy, she always has to outdo everyone else."

"That's it!" shouted Kimberly. She did a few ballet leaps ahead, gracefully sailing over a low bench.

"That's what?" asked Winnie.

"That's how I'll get out of having to perform for the *Week at the U.*"

"I don't follow," said Faith.

"Look." Kimberly leapt up on the seat of a long, wooden bench and sat on the backrest. "Liza understudied for me in The Follies and was a raging success."

"Don't remind me," Faith said.

"So," said Kimberly, "I'll just ask Liza to dance "Magician at Midnight" for me."

"Liza as Merlin the Magician?" said Winnie. "I can't picture that. Maybe she could be the eye of the newt or the tongue of the toad."

"Kimberly, that is just about the worst idea you've ever had," Faith laughed.

"No," said Kimberly, jumping down from the bench. "Telling my Mom I'm performing was the worst idea I've ever had. She's called every day to grill me about my routine. What music am I using? What steps? You'd think I was appearing on Broadway."

"Forget about Liza," said Winnie. "I'll dance for you." She spun around in a few awkward twirls. Her long, peasant skirt ballooned out, exposing her flower printed tights. "You will follow me," she said, swirling her hands in mysterious magical movements, dancing backward, pulling Kimberly and Faith after her. They followed, whooping and yelling all the way to the gym, where a banner hung from the top of the building.

Emanuel Roberts Gymnasium
Fencing Demonstration—Aquanauts
Tonight 8:00

They joined the line filing into the building. Most of the crowd walking in with them turned left down the hall to the swimming pool. Winnie wrinkled her nose at the strong smell of chlorine. "If fencing gets boring," she whispered, "we can go watch the water ballet demonstration."

"Fencing wasn't too popular at my school," said Kimberly, stretching her long legs in front of her to smooth out the wrinkles in her tights. "The only reason we had fencing was because an alum donated the equipment and paid for a coach. I liked it because there's precise movement involved."

Winnie laughed. "You have to be precise if you're going to strike your opponent before he strikes you."

They rounded a corner and entered the main gymnasium.

At eight o'clock sharp, a slender, but powerfully

built woman walked out onto the gym floor and approached the stands. Her short, curly, black hair glistened under the harsh, gym lights. She carried a sword in one hand and thickly padded gloves in the other. Her fencing mask was braced under her arm. A vest protected her body.

"She looks like a Ninja Turtle," said Winnie, folding a piece of gum into her mouth.

"That's Madeline Golden," Kimberly said. "She fenced for the United States in the Olympics. My high school had a film of that team. Wait till you see her in action."

"Thank you all for coming this evening," said Madeline Golden, standing directly in front of the girls. "Since there are so few of you here tonight, I think it might be best if everyone moves into this section. That way we can direct the action a little better."

People slid over from the sides and walked down from the upper rows. Then the audience applauded politely as six students walked to the middle of the gym. They all wore protective gear and each carried a thick, black, mesh mask tucked under one arm, and a sword in the other.

"You're right," Kimberly whispered to Winnie. "They do look like Ninja Turtles. This sport will never be the same for me again."

"As they go through their paces," Ms. Golden said, "I'll explain what they're doing and I'll fill you in on a bit of fencing history."

The duelers paired up and began the intricate movements of the duel. The vests of the pair closest to the audience were hooked up to a system that lit a red light when a sword point touched an opponent. As the demonstration went on, the pair became more and more active, attacking and retreating, attacking again.

"They're good," said Kimberly.

"They look like Josh and me fighting in the dining commons," said Winnie.

"Maybe you should borrow one of those vests for the All Dorm Pizza Party," said Faith. "That way you'll be protected if Josh tries to break your heart again."

"I have a better idea," said Winnie. "I'll bring one of those swords along."

"They're called épées," said Kimberly. "I mean, if you're going to run the poor guy through, you should at least know the name of the thing you're doing it with."

"Good point. I'll say, here's your pepperoni pizza Mr. Josh Gaffey, and oh, by the way, *en guarde.*" Winnie jumped up, swinging an imaginary épée over her head.

"Perfect timing," said Ms. Golden, coming over to Winnie. "I was just about to ask for a volunteer for the next demonstration."

"But I—" started Winnie.

"Come on," said the instructor, smiling, waving Winnie out to the floor.

"Oh, hold on now," said Winnie. "You've got the wrong person. With my luck, I'll stab my own foot."

Ms. Golden laughed, her eyes scanning the audience. "Well, I need someone who is confident physically but has never fenced with anyone on the team before."

"Here she is!" said Winnie, grabbing Kimberly's arm, tugging her up.

Kimberly pulled back. "I can't," she said.

"Come on, Kimberly," urged Faith, "It will be good practice performing in front of crowds."

"Right," said Winnie, pushing Kimberly down the row, "and it's not like you have to do a whole dance or anything."

Reluctantly, Kimberly stepped out onto the gym floor. One of the varsity fencers started taking off her gear to give to Kimberly.

"Let's give our volunteer a hand," said Golden. The small audience applauded as she helped Kimberly buckle the vest and adjust the mask.

Kimberly tugged on the gloves. She felt the heft of the épée in her hand, then turned menacingly to her friends. "You got me into this," she said. "I'll get even." Faith and Winnie clutched each other in mock horror. "When you least expect it," warned Kimberly. She sliced a Zorro "Z" in the air.

"The purpose of this part of our demonstration," said Ms. Golden, readjusting a couple of the straps on Kimberly's vest, "is to show how two fencers who have never faced each other before learn to read each other's bodies and moves." She looked toward the back of the gym where the rest of the fencing team waited. "Can one of you please step up?" she said. A student trotted out from the pack, mask down, gloves on, épée ready.

The metal tongue holding the mask on pressed into the back of Kimberly's head. She wished she had the equipment she'd used all through high school. This equipment felt ill-fitting and awkward, as if she had put on someone else's toe shoes. Kimberly shifted the mask, trying to make it more comfortable. The good thing about the thick mesh was that it hid her face completely and kept her from feeling totally exposed.

"Fencing with someone is very much like dancing with them," Ms. Golden explained to the audience.

"You've seen me dance," yelled a guy from the audience.

Ms. Golden laughed along with the crowd. "Except," she said, "in a real duel, a person's life depends on how well he or she leads and follows." She stood between Kimberly and the other fencer like a referee at a prize fight. "Now," she continued, "what I'd like you two to start with is . . ."

As she described the first few moves, Kimberly watched the other person. Her nervousness disappeared as she concentrated on her opponent. She'd towered over all the students on her high school team. This opponent was bigger and taller than anyone she'd had to duel before.

"All right," said the instructor, stepping back. "You two may begin whenever you're ready."

Holding her upper body steady, Kimberly bent at the knees, held her left arm back and up, and eased her body forward. She circled her opponent, keeping him at a distance, carefully sizing up his movements, aggressiveness, personality. She was a panther on the scent of her prey. Graceful, powerful, she made little circles with the épée, testing his rhythm. They moved like dancers, flowing together, finding the right pacing and tension, each waiting for the other to take the lead.

Now! thought Kimberly.

"Ooohhhh," said the crowd as Kimberly parried and thrust. The other person didn't flinch. "Ahh-hhh," said the crowd as he parried, coming at her with speed and grace. Kimberly easily sidestepped the attack. *He's good,* she thought. *This could be difficult.*

Thoughts of the crowd fell away as Kimberly concentrated on her opponent's moves. She held the hilt snug against her hand, feeling the sword become an extension of her arm.

He attacked and she retreated. She attacked and he moved aside. Action and reaction, give and take. When she was totally in sync with an opponent, the way she was now, there was a magical chemistry. Fencing could be as sensual as dancing, with the added element of danger thrown in. Kimberly had forgotten how much she liked fencing. Maybe she'd join the U. of S. team. Maybe . . .

Her vest strap loosened suddenly, distracting her for a moment. Her opponent attacked. She flinched as his large body flew at her, moving with speed and grace, his épée cutting the air around her, the thin blade whistling past her ear. She struggled as her vest slid around. Couldn't he see that she was in trouble? Why didn't he stop?

The crowd gasped.

"Look out," someone shouted.

"Attack!" someone else hollered.

Before Kimberly could react, her opponent's swift lunge caught her off guard and sent her flying. Her épée flew out of her hand, clattering along the gym floor as she crashed to the ground. Kimberly looked up at the sea of strange faces staring at her. Sounds of the room rushed in at her.

"She's hurt."

"Did he stab her?"

Through the thick mask she saw people jumping off the benches to come to her aid. Her heart beat like a trapped bird against the vest. She wanted to disappear. Shocked and embarrassed, she burst into angry tears. Suddenly, strong arms scooped her up and carried her out, into the gym supply room. It was her opponent. He kicked aside basketballs, volleyballs, and other loose equipment, setting her down on a stack of gym mats. Madeline Golden followed from the gym.

"Are you all right?" she asked.

"I'm fine," said Kimberly.

"I think her pride's hurt more than anything," said her opponent.

Faith and Winnie ran in. "You okay?" they both asked, as they stood over her.

Kimberly felt the small space closing in around her. She nodded. "I'm all right," she said.

"Come on, girls," said Ms. Golden. "Why don't we give her time to catch her breath."

"You sure you're not hurt?" asked Winnie.

"I'm sure. Honest."

"Let's go back and finish the demonstration," said Ms. Golden, shooing Faith and Winnie back into the gym. "I'll see you a little later, Kimberly."

Kimberly pulled off her mask, rubbing the sore spot where the metal tongue had dug into her head. Her opponent knelt beside her.

"Sorry about that," he said, working off his mask.

"You!" Kimberly stared at Derek Weldon. Her physics lab partner's dark eyes sparkled. His smirking half-smile made him seem even more arrogant than the day they'd met in the lab. What was it about him that turned her emotions inside out? "You," she said, again, anger washing over her.

"Me," he said.

"Where'd you learn to fence?" She yanked off her gloves, wiping her moist hands on her vest. "Friday night wrestling?"

"What'd I do?" he asked defensively.

"That was unsportsman like," began Kimberly. "You don't take advantage of an opponent like that."

"Hey," said Derek, looking hurt. "I didn't do it on purpose."

"I'll bet." A week ago she didn't know Derek Weldon. Now, all of a sudden, he showed up everywhere, messing up her life.

"You're right," he said. He unclasped his vest and pulled it off, hanging it over a nearby weight bar. He sat next to her on the mats. "I wasn't concentrating as much as I should have. It's all this pressure. I'm not thinking straight."

"I told you in lab that we're all under pressure." Kimberly hugged her knees to her chest, stretching out her sore back muscles. "You can't go around putting a sword in your hand and not be thinking about the person you're aiming it at."

"Hey. Lighten up. I admitted you were right."

Kimberly felt perspiration running down her temples. There was no way she'd join the fencing team as long as he was on it. Unless, of course, they'd let her run him through with her sword.

"Mind telling me what happened out there?" he asked, pulling a handkerchief out of his pocket. He pressed the cloth against her forehead. His gentle concern surprised her. It didn't go with the rest of him.

His dark, sparkling eyes stared at her. Kimberly swallowed. In all the years she'd dated Boring Mark Frazier, he never once looked at her this way. It was as if Mark Frazier was a slow freight train and Derek Weldon was the superexpress. He reached over, resting his strong hand on her shoulder. His fingers seemed to burn through her shirt.

Kimberly shifted uneasily, not sure what was happening to her. "Why didn't you back off when you saw me in trouble?" she asked.

"I didn't notice . . . I mean, I'd never . . . That is, I'm usually careful when . . ." Derek sighed. "It's not true. The fact is, I'm always running three steps ahead of where I should be," he said. "And right now, I'm a little more crazed than usual. Want to hear what's going on in my life?"

"Not particularly," said Kimberly.

He curled out his lower lip, pouting. "Oh. How about telling me your sad story if I can tell you mine."

"That's fair." The muffled sound of applause went up inside the gym.

"Is it over?" asked Kimberly.

"No. That was the junior exhibition. You're not

going to get away from me that easily." He retied his shoelaces. "Aside from fencing practice, I have two term papers due, three tests to study for, two more *Week at the U* events I'm supposed to participate in. And, my biggest problem—aside from you," his smile surprised her, sending unexpected chills down her body, "is that I'm supposed to do a science demonstration for a group of little kids next Wednesday for my education class."

"*You* are studying to be a teacher?" Kimberly couldn't help laughing. "Oh, those poor kids."

"Thanks for your support," he said. "I thought I could do the demonstration. No sweat. But it looks like this time I've really bitten off a whole lot more than I can chew."

His eyes held hers like a magnet. She couldn't look away if she wanted to—and she didn't want to. She shifted, wincing at the sharp pain in her back.

"What's wrong?" Derek asked.

"I must have done something to my back when I fell."

Kimberly rolled onto her knees, arching her back into a cat's cradle. A dull pain at the base of her spine spread out into her hips.

"Maybe you'd better walk it out." Derek stood, holding out a hand to help her up.

She slid her hands into his, feeling his strong fingers close around hers. He pulled her up gently, easily, as if she were feather-light. For a moment they stood face to face and Kimberly felt the walls of the small room closing in on her. A tingle ran across her shoulders and down her back. She forced herself to step away from him to safer ground.

"You okay?" he asked.

She bent forward, backward, sideways, checking her legs, hips, back, and arms. "My hip's sore, but nothing seems to be broken."

"That's a start."

They walked around and around the small area, weaving in and out of free weights, basketballs, volleyballs, bright orange cones, and other equipment littering the floor. Every now and then Kimberly leaned against the wall, stretching out the muscles in her back. She had experienced enough dancer's kinks and knots over the years to know this wasn't serious. Still, it was nice walking alongside Derek. She liked the fact that he seemed concerned about her.

"So," she said, "what kind of science demonstrations are you doing with the little kids?"

"That's the problem," he said. "I can't come up with an idea that's good enough. This is my first time in front of a real live class and I want it to be spectacular."

"Spectacular?" Kimberly picked up a couple of two-pound hand weights, lifting them up and down as she walked, letting them pull gently on her back muscles. "How about blowing up the classroom?"

"Ho, ho, ho," he said. "Any other ideas?"

"Just go to the library and open some books. You'll find a million and one ideas for your demonstration."

"Who has time to go to the library?"

"Well, at least it would help you. I, on the other hand," she said, "have to perform next Wednesday in front of an auditorium full of people. And I have no one who can help me."

She stopped walking. Holding the weights down in front of her, she slowly bent forward from the waist until the weights rested on the floor.

"Are you talking about that dance performance you mentioned the other day?"

"Yes," she said. *So, he listened to me when we fought in the physics lab. Maybe Derek isn't totally insensitive.* "Seems to me I've been preparing for this moment since I was a kid."

"How can you concentrate on one thing like

that?" He smiled. "If I don't have five things going all the time, I think I'm being lazy."

Kimberly leaned against the wall. "My whole life has been dance. My mom runs a dance troupe." She began gathering her fencing gear. "Of course, I'll probably get so sick to my stomach with stage fright that I won't even be able to make an entrance." Another round of applause drifted in from the gym.

"The audience didn't seem to bother you when we were fencing," Derek said, picking up his gear.

"That was different."

"An audience is an audience."

"Not when you're dancing in a spotlight, putting your heart and soul into your movements. Besides, I was concentrating on you, what you were doing. I forgot about all those people staring at me."

Derek walked her to the door. Just as he was about to push it open for her, he stopped and stared at her. Kimberly tried not to look into his eyes, tried not to think about the funny little leaps her heart was taking. She had enough to worry about without adding a romance with a scatterbrain—even a cute, interesting, talented scatterbrain. Martin Frazier and his predictable boring letters were as much romance as she could handle right now.

"Can I call you later?" asked Derek. "See how you're feeling?"

Kimberly couldn't read the expression in his eyes, and she ignored the warning bells in her heart. "I guess that would be all right."

"Good." He reached over her head and pushed open the gym door.

They walked in together, just as the demonstration was ending. Derek left to take his bows with the rest of the team. Kimberly liked the proud way he stood in line, and didn't take her eyes off him as the team filed out of the gym.

"Kimberly!" She was only dimly aware of Faith and Winnie clamoring down the rows of benches toward her.

Kimberly stood staring after Derek. Something had just happened to her but, as hard as she tried, she couldn't figure out how to describe it to anyone, let alone herself. Somehow, even with all her bruises and aches, she felt better than she had in a very long time.

Nine

KC and Peter walked hand in hand into the elegant glass and chrome lobby of the Garland Building. Large crowds blocked the elevators. Men in elegant suits and women in silk dresses pushed the buttons impatiently, nervously glancing at their watches.

"Morning rush hour," said Peter.

KC checked her watch. Five minutes to nine. Five minutes until she was due to walk into the Adela Loomis modeling agency. "I'll be late for my appointment!"

"Will you please stop worrying?" He pulled her off to a quiet corner.

KC checked herself in the mirrored wall. Peter

stood behind her, smiling, his hair flopping over his forehead, his faded football jersey out of place in the professional building. KC tried to smile, to let him know she was all right, but she wasn't. She was a wreck.

Peter bent over and kissed her neck. "Last night you wouldn't let me take you out for coffee after the lecture," he said. "And this morning you barely touched your breakfast." He stroked his hand along her hair. "You're going to make yourself sick."

"I'm just so nervous," she said, checking her makeup one last time.

"You look sensational," said Peter. "Stop worrying."

KC reapplied some raspberry lipstick. "Do you think this lipstick's too dark?"

"It's perfect."

Next she took out her hair pick, trying to add more fullness into the mass of dark curls at the crown. "My hair's horrible."

"It's *perfect!*"

"Why does hair always do weird things exactly when you need it to look great?"

"I give up," he said, nuzzling her neck. "Your hair looks awful, your makeup is terrible, and you have pimples breaking out all over your face."

"Thanks, Dvorsky," said KC, wiggling her nose at him. "I feel much better now. They're just going to hate me. What made me think I could do this? I don't know the first thing about being a professional model."

Four elevators came at once, taking most of the waiting crowd. "This car next," said the uniformed guard.

"You're sure you don't want me to come up with you?" asked Peter.

"Positive," said KC, suddenly feeling shaky all over. "I don't even want to go up."

Peter slung his camera bag over his shoulder and, taking firm hold of KC's arm, led her to the end elevator. "You will go up and you will be great! Promise you'll call me as soon as you're through?"

"Promise. Unless, of course, they send me out on a job immediately. Bathing suits in Bora Bora. Gowns in Gibraltar."

"Call," he said, not moving until she stepped into an elevator and the doors slid closed.

I will be calm, KC thought, as she squished in the middle of the crowd. She tried to distract herself by thinking about Peter, his sweet smile, his relaxed style, but, as the elevator traveled up, KC couldn't calm down.

She was still a bundle of nerves when she walked into the Adela Loomis office. For a moment, she thought she had stepped into the court of Louis XIV. The walls were wallpapered with an ornate design, and urns of plumes stood in the corners.

"Be there in a moment," sang a voice from the back. "Just make yourself comfortable."

KC closed the door softly behind her, tiptoeing across the deep royal blue carpet to look at the photos of famous movie stars that filled one entire wall. "To Adela with love, Kim Basinger." "For Adela, the miracle worker, Demi Moore." "Nobody does it better, Hugs and Kisses, Bernadette Peters." "Hey, Adela, thanks for everything! Bette."

KC sat on the edge of a huge straight-back chair and set her briefcase next to her. Inside were more copies of the photos she'd already sent to the agency, just in case they wanted extras. Two of the photos were from the Classic Calendar shoot Peter had done. He had also made up a composite sheet for her, printing four different poses of her on the front and, on the back, listing her name, phone, address, and physical statistics including dress and shoe size.

"All the models have these," he'd explained. "The agency makes copies and sends them to advertising companies. That way you don't have to waste your time running to a job audition that's hiring three-foot blonds."

KC had thought Peter's photos would be a great way to show modeling agents all the different looks she could do. Now she wasn't so sure. Staring at Adela Loomis' wall of movie stars and famous models, KC wondered if she should have sent the photos at all.

"Thank you so very much for waiting," said the woman whisking into the room. KC stared as the brassy blond carried a tiny Pekingese dog to the desk and sat down.

"I'm—"

"Yes, yes, one moment, dear," said the woman, stroking the dog on her lap, and shuffling through the mess of papers on her ornately carved desk. "Ah, yes, here we are." Adela held up the packet of photos KC had mailed in along with the composite sheet Peter had made. She brushed cookie crumbs off of it. KC saw coffee cup rings around the bottom. She hoped the photos weren't ruined. Even with Peter making copies in his dorm darkroom, the film and originals had cost a small fortune. The woman put on a pair of diamond-studded half-glasses and peered down at her notes. "You are Kay?"

"KC," said KC. "Actually, my name is Kahia Cayanne."

"Why that's lovely," gushed the woman. "Why-*ever* would you want to change it to something so mun*dane* as KC?"

"Well, I just thought—"

"Nonsense. To be a truly great model, you must do *every*thing possible to stand *out* in a crowd. Just look at my friends," she waved her hand to the wall of photos. "Bernadette. Bette. Madonna. Twiggy. Cher. If you didn't have a name like—like —what was that again, dear?"

"Kahia Cayanne." It was an unwanted birth gift from her hippy parents.

"Right. If you didn't have *that* name, I would have to in*vent* one for you." She stuck a long, tan cigarette into an even longer mother-of-pearl holder and flicked open a gold lighter. "You can hardly expect clients to pay sixty and seventy dollars an hour for a model named KC. But Kahia Cayanne . . ." She dragged deeply on the cigarette, exhaling the smoke in a thin stream toward the ceiling. "My, my, my, a name like *that* might command a hundred dollars or more an hour."

KC swallowed, confused. *How could a woman who looked like Adela, whose office was not in Los Angeles or New York, know all those famous people? She must be very good. A hundred dollars an hour!* If KC worked only a couple of hours a week, she could pay for the Tri Beta dues increase, and have a fortune left over for tutors, clothing, and all sorts of things.

"Have you worked with all these stars?" asked KC.

Adela waved the back of her hand at the photos. "My children," she said. "I don't like to brag, my dear. Nor do I like to dwell on the past. But remember, every great star, every great model, was once an unknown waiting to be discovered. First, must come the desire." She leaned forward, knocking over a box of paper clips. "Do you have that, Kaheea? Do you have that *special* desire?"

"I—I think—"

"Don't think!" She slammed her jeweled hand on the desk. The dog yelped and jumped off her lap. "A great model does not *think* she is great. She *knows* it. Do you *feel* greatness inside yourself, Kahana? Do you feel that special star quality welling up from deep inside?"

"Well," KC swallowed. "I think, that is, I'm really interested in business. But there have been times, over the years, that I've wondered if I should try modeling. I mean—"

"Stand up, stand up, my dear. Let's have a

look." KC stood. "Ah, yes. Um-hum." Adela walked slowly around her. "Stand straight. Straighter. Well, we can work on that. And your hair. Tsk. Tsk. That will take some doing. Your makeup is, of course, all wrong for your coloring. And I don't know what we'll be able to do with your shoulders. Scoliosis?"

"No, I never—"

"Not everyone who has it *knows* they have it, my dear. Trust me, your spine is something we need to work on. We can perform miracles with the right exercise. And the correct clothing can camouflage all sorts of nature's little mistakes."

KC felt close to tears. How could all her friends say she was beautiful? Why had she listened to them? Adela, who had no reason to lie, was telling her the truth.

"I . . . I'm sorry to have taken up your time," she said reaching across the desk for her photos, and putting them back into their manila envelope. After all the time she spent getting ready for this interview, all the money she spent mailing her photos and composites, this wasn't what she had expected. No one needed to be humiliated this way. She wouldn't even bother with the other interview at Springfield Faces.

"My dear child," said Adela, a sudden sharpness to her voice. "What*ever* are you doing?"

"Going home. I don't know what made me think I could model."

"Sit down, sit down, don't be foolish." She waved KC back into the chair. "Just because someone brings me a lump of clay, doesn't mean I can't shape it. You have good bone structure, a certain look. Given time and hard work—"

"But I need money now," said KC. "If I can't model, I'll have to find another job."

For some reason, Adela found this amusing. "Ha, ha, ha, my dear, someone who can afford a cashmere sweater like the one you're wearing, and that hand-tooled, Italian leather briefcase, is hardly starving. Ha, ha. I promise, after the few months you spend taking my course—"

"Course?" said KC, suddenly on guard.

"Adela Loomis's Famous Modeling Course. Where do you think all these famous people began? You think Christie Brinkley just hopped up onto a runway and was discovered? No, dear Kalenna, it started right *here*. Three nights a week, for three months, for three hundred dollars. Then, *then,* the world of modeling will begin to open for you."

KC had enough business sense to know a hustle

when she heard one. She may have felt miserable a few minutes ago, but anger cleared her mind.

"And if I'm not good enough to model in three months?" asked KC.

"Don't be negative, dear," smiled Adela, as if she'd hooked her fish. "I will, of course, continue to work with you as long as it takes."

"For an additional fee?"

The smile on the woman's face was not quite so friendly. "You can hardly expect my quality services to come free."

KC's heart raced. She should have treated this whole modeling business like a real business from the beginning. Why had she come in here like a child with stars in her eyes? Why hadn't she called the Better Business Bureau to see if anyone had made a complaint against the Adela Loomis modeling agency?

"For your information, Miss Loomis, this isn't my cashmere sweater. In fact, it probably cost as much as my entire wardrobe for the year." KC stood and jammed her photos back into the briefcase, zipping it closed. "And this briefcase was a high school graduation present from my family. They're still paying off the store where they bought it."

The smile was definitely gone from Adela

Loomis's mouth. Without it, her over-painted face was mean and hard. "Well then, Karmeena, I wish you luck in what*ever* you choose to do with your life. I am just sorry you will never make it as a model."

KC stormed out of the office. She jammed her finger into the elevator button. What a rip-off. The only person getting work from the Adela Loomis Modeling Agency was Adela Loomis. *How many poor kids threw their money away on that scam? Well, not KC Angeletti.*

The elevator doors opened and she stepped on. She'd call and cancel her appointment with Springfield Faces. No one was going to take advantage of her again. She remembered her father's words: If you fool me once, shame on you. If you fool me twice, shame on me.

No one was going to fool her twice. In fact, even better than calling, she'd keep her appointment at Springfield Faces. She'd go there to pick up her packet of photos and at the same time tell them face-to-face what she thought of their bogus operation. *Lookout Springfield Faces,* she thought as she stormed off the elevator and out of the building. *Here comes KC Angeletti.*

Ten

· · · · · · · · · · · · · · ·

"Yes," said the girl. She sobbed, gazing off to the left. "They told me you were *fools.*" She wrung her hands. "That I should not *listen* to your kind words. Nor *trust* in your charity."

Faith winced as Joan of Arc overacted on the portable stage at the front of the classroom. Not that Faith could have done any better. But why did every other girl in her Acting 101 class pick this same scene from George Bernard Shaw's play?

Half the class slept, while the other half doodled. Liza was slumped in the chair next to Faith. "If I hear this scene one more time," she whispered, "I'm going to give up acting and become a monk."

"Bread *has* no *sor*row for me." The girl fell to her knees. "Water no af*flic*tion. But to shut me off from the light of day—"

Last week, Faith performed a scene from *Our Town,* for this five minute monologue assignment. She prayed none of the good actors in the class would select the same scene. As bad as her acting was, it would look worse next to a really good performance. So far, she'd been lucky.

Joan of Arc finished the scene, rolled to the edge of the stage, and flopped off, laying motionless on the floor. "I can't tell if she's emoting or if she fainted," said Liza. "Maybe if she fainted, we'll get a five minute break."

"All right, good" said Mr. Francosi, jumping up from his seat. "Thank you Miss Gill. Now, can we move all the chairs back into three rows?" he said. "We'll finish up with fifteen minutes of improv."

Chairs squeaked along the floor, people moved their book bags and coats back to clear the center of the room. "Hey, Faith," said her new roommate, "do you know when that All Dorm Pizza Party is?"

"Tomorrow night," answered Faith. "Eight o'clock."

"Think we should invite Christopher Hammond?" asked Liza.

"*Week at the U* events are open to everyone," said Faith, pulling back two chairs at once while Liza looked on. "Anyway, I'm sure he'll be there with his TV crew."

"Still," said Liza, watching Faith work, "it might be nice if we asked him."

Francosi scanned the class. Faith slunk lower. "Who wants to start?" he asked.

"Me!" Liza jumped up and jogged to the front of the room. Francosi fanned out a stack of index cards. "Pick one," he said. Liza closed her eyes and tugged a card from the middle of the deck. "Turn it over and read your scene. But don't tell us what it is you're doing. We'll have to guess."

Liza turned the card over. "Oh, no!" she said, bugging out her eyes and crossing them. "I don't want to do this!" A few kids laughed. They thought Liza was funny. *That,* thought Faith, *was because they didn't have to room with her.*

"You're stuck with it," said Francosi. Taking out a stopwatch he said, "You have fifteen seconds to prepare, two minutes to perform. Go!"

Liza turned her back to the audience, composing her scene. Slowly, she started curling up, smaller and smaller. When she finally turned toward the audience, she'd changed into a five-year-old child, a child riding in the back of a car, a child riding in the back of a car who had to go to the bathroom. The class roared as Liza added layer on layer, miming, mugging.

How did Liza do it? How could she stand right in front of a group of people and dive head first into a character? Faith could never let go like that. Liza Ruff might be the world's most annoying roommate, but there was no denying she had talent. Two quick improvs followed Liza's. Neither was nearly as good.

Near the end of class, Francosi announced their assignment for the following week. "We need to work some more on motivation," he said. The class groaned. "I know it's hard. But if you don't know *why* your character is doing something, you'll never get your audience to believe." He took a bunch of papers out of his briefcase. "I am assigning all of you the same monologue. But you will each be given a different motivation."

"What do you mean?" someone asked.

"You can read exactly the same words in different ways. Everything depends on what your character wants. Here," he said, putting down the stack of papers. "I'll show you. Let's do a lover and killer."

He jumped off the stage, strode to Faith, and took her hand in his. "You are mine," he said, with such tenderness that Faith felt her face burn with embarrassment. Then Francosi let go of her hand and turned his back on her. When he turned again his face was contorted with hatred. "You," he said, his quiet voice dripping with bone-chilling evil, "are mine." Faith stared at him. How did he make both seem so real? Any audience would believe either reading.

"See?" asked Francosi. "My first objective was to make you love me. My second was to frighten you. Same words. Two different motivations. Any questions?" He picked up the papers again. "All right, here's the scene. I've written a different motivation on the top of each sheet, and—"

Just then the classroom door opened and Christopher Hammond strolled in.

"What's he doing here?" Faith muttered. Old anger sprung up inside of her. First he barged in on poor Kimberly's dance rehearsal and now here he was invading Acting 101. Why was Christopher suddenly turning up everywhere in her life? She fumed as the ever-cool Christopher walked over to Francosi. "At least this time he didn't drag along a camera crew," she said to Liza.

"Not yet," said Liza, smiling mysteriously.

"Yes?" asked Francosi.

"Sorry to interrupt," said Christopher, brushing a lock of blond hair off his forehead. "I'm a student at U. of S., and also an intern with KRUS news. I'd like to tape this class next Wednesday for a segment I'm doing on the *Week at the U.*"

No! thought Faith.

"Sure," said Francosi. "Hey, class," he said, "it looks like you're getting your chance to be famous for fifteen minutes." He shook hands with Christopher. "How'd you hear about us?"

Christopher turned his totally charming and totally phony smile toward the class. "One of your students, Liza Ruff, thought a beginning acting class might make lively footage."

"We'll do our best," said Francosi.

Faith gritted her teeth as Christopher walked out of the room. He made her want to throw up. It was miserable enough to have to get up in front of this class and try to act. But how could she do it in front of Christopher and his slimy smile and better-than-thou attitude? She grabbed a scene sheet from Francosi on her way out of class and shoved it into her notebook.

"Hey," Liza called out, running after her. Faith ignored her. She was furious at Liza for doing this. "Look." Liza waved her sheet at Faith. "My objective is to amuse."

Amuse? thought Faith. *That's the only thing she knows how to do. But the way I feel right now, nothing could amuse me—especially not Liza Ruff.*

"What'd you get?" asked Liza.

Faith pulled her sheet out of her notebook and glanced down at the words Mr. Francosi had scrawled across the top. A knot twisted in her stomach. *This can't be happening. There's no way I can read this scene in front of the class.* Liza tore the sheet out of her hand. Faith kept walking, ignoring Liza's "Oooh la la" and rude laugh.

The objective of Faith's reading to the class *and* Christopher *and* all his cameras, was . . . to seduce.

Eleven

"**K**imberly," yelled Winnie. She stood near the front doors, under the All Dorm Pizza Party sign, waving wildly. "Over here."

Kimberly waved back, making it through the crowd to her friends just as the eight o'clock chimes sounded. The doors opened and students yelling "Piz-za! Piz-za!" surged through the dorm's huge lobby toward the food.

"Maybe we should wait until the crowd thins out," Faith shouted.

"You kidding?" yelled Winnie who had dyed the tips of her hair purple in honor of the party. "If we wait, there won't be any pizza left. Our food committee already ate half of them while they were setting up."

Toilet paper streamers hung from overhead pipes and paper cups were glued into designs on the windows. Black balloons, half of them popped or deflating, were taped to the walls. The girls finally made their way to the front where a line of Forest Hall jocks worked the pizza table. Wearing neon *Week at the U* T-shirts, laughing, joking, and shouting, they plunked limp slices of pizza onto the girls' flimsy paper plates.

"Let's find a quieter place," Faith shouted.

Kimberly looked over the crowd. "There's a space," she said. "Follow me." All of them walked over to the table Kimberly had spotted and sat down.

"It just looks so *high school,*" said KC, opening several napkins on her lap to keep the pizza grease from soaking through her plate to her skirt. "Why did I ever think college was going to be super sophisticated? Peter should be here to capture this historical moment on film."

"I bet he went home for the weekend just so he wouldn't have to eat this." Winnie lifted the cheese off the top of her pepperoni pizza. The slice was so cold the cheese had hardened into a solid sheet.

"That looks like the wax the orthodontist used to give me," said Faith. "You know the stuff. You break off little pieces and stick them on the sharp ends so they don't cut the insides of your mouth."

"The veggie pizza's not much better," Kimberly said, holding up her slice. "If I'm lucky, I'll get food poisoning and be too sick to perform." She bit into the pizza, the burnt crust raining crumbs all over her black cat suit.

"Looks like you need a good vacuuming," said a male voice.

Her teeth clamped on the pizza, Kimberly rolled her eyes up as Derek walked past with a group of friends. She held her breath, hoping for an instant, that he would stay and talk. But his eyes swept over her friends and she could tell he'd be uncomfortable invading their all-girl crowd. He winked at her, leaving before she could think of anything to say.

"Ooooohhhhh, Kimberly," the girls swooned together.

Embarrassed, Kimberly dropped the pizza back on the plate and tried to brush the crumbs off her outfit.

"Wasn't that the guy at the fencing demonstration?" asked Faith.

"He got me!" gasped Winnie. She clutched her hands to her chest and fell back on the floor. "One stab, straight through the heart."

Faith picked the green peppers off her pizza. "I'll bet *he's* not boring."

"That's for sure." Kimberly stretched her long legs in front of her and flexed her feet, pointing her toes up at the ceiling then down toward the floor. "But I can't figure out exactly what Derek Weldon is. Intellectual? Jock? Scatterbrain?"

One thing she *did* know for sure, Derek was not a thing in the world like Martin Frazier. Martin's boring form letters came like clockwork, beautifully written on expensive, tan paper. Kimberly didn't think Derek was the type who would write the same letter twice.

"Well, I've dated exciting and I've dated boring," said Faith. "And it seems to me that the one good thing about a boring boyfriend is that you always know where you stand."

"Yeah," said Winnie, "you're always standing still."

The girls laughed, taking punch cups from a tray being passed by a party hostess. The volume and beat of the music cranked up and more people started dancing.

"I love this song," said Winnie, jumping up, dancing by herself.

"There's Josh," said KC.

Winnie stopped dancing. "Where?"

"Dancing with that blond over there."

Winnie put her hands on her hips. "You call that dancing?"

She brushed off her polka-dotted skirt and tightened her neon boot laces. "I'll show you some serious dancing." She grabbed Sean Mark, the football player who lived two doors down from her.

"Hey, I can't dance," he protested.

"You keep me up all night with your wild parties," said Winnie. "You owe me big. Now dance!" She pulled him out onto the dance floor.

Kimberly, Faith and KC looked on as Winnie walked out onto the floor. The second Josh saw her, he started dancing harder and faster.

"Dueling dancers," said Faith, tucking her hands into the sides of her overalls.

"How can those two be so public about their emotions?" asked KC, blotting the corners of her mouth with her napkin. "They fight in public and make up in public. It's like watching 'The Winnie and Josh Show.' "

"I don't get it," said Faith. "Why do two people who really want to be together always wind up doing things that keep them apart?"

"Wouldn't it be great if we had some magical way of sticking Winnie and Josh together until they get straightened out?" said Kimberly.

They watched Winnie dancing wildly on the floor, skirt flying, bracelets jangling. Muscle-bound Sean Mark could barely move his feet. "He looks like a dancing bear," said Kimberly. "Poor Winnie."

"Poor Winnie did this to herself," said KC. "What about poor *me?* I've got to go to that modeling agency on Wednesday and demand my photos back." She shivered. "I just know the people at Springfield Faces are going to be every bit as yucky as Adela Loomis."

"Poor *me,*" said Faith, as she stood up. She folded her pizza crusts in the paper plate. "I've got to go rehearse my monologue for acting class. Can you picture me, Faith Behind-the-Scenes Crowley, standing in front of the world, playing a character who's trying to *seduce?*"

Kimberly and KC looked at Faith, at her girl-next-door features and down-to-earth overalls, at her little girl freckles and practical braid. "No," they said together.

"Come on." KC stood, brushing crumbs from her skirt, rebuttoning her blazer, "I'll walk with you."

"You don't have to leave early because of me," said Faith.

"This isn't really my kind of party," said KC, ducking a piece of falling toilet paper, and stepping over a half-eaten slab of pizza. "I'm not used to all this wonderful elegance. Besides, I've really got to get back to my dorm and study."

"You coming, Kim?" asked Faith.

Kimberly leaned against a wall, watching Winnie out of one eye, keeping tabs on Derek with the other. Her homework could wait. She wasn't ready to go back to her dorm. "You go ahead," she said. "I'll keep tabs on Winnie. She may need a shoulder to cry on later."

As soon as her friends left, Kimberly ducked into the ladies room. The last time she'd seen Derek, she'd been all sweaty from the fencing face mask. Well, this time she planned to be ready. Taking a few minutes to put on her face, as her mother called it, might be just the action she needed to get a reaction out of her lab partner.

Setting her little makeup bag on the counter,

Kimberly took a long hard look at herself. *Derek Weldon,* she thought, *you are not leaving this party without spending at least a few minutes with me. I don't know how I'm going to do it, but I am a determined woman.*

Her eyes, she decided, could do with some eye shadow, liner, and mascara. Then she dabbed a little blush on her cheekbones, and finished off with the new Kissable Kopper lipstick she'd bought. She felt like her "Magician at Midnight," mixing up potions to get what she wanted. Poor Derek. He didn't have a chance of escape.

Twelve

·····················

"**O**ne or two slices?" Phoenix shouted.

"One," said Courtney. She stood off to one side of the Forest Hall lobby, out of the way of the hungry masses crowding around the pizza table.

"How many?" he called over the blaring music.

"One." Then, realizing he couldn't hear her, she held up one finger. He smiled and dove back into the pizza line.

Courtney could barely breathe. There was no air circulating in the overcrowded room. The All Dorm Pizza Party was more like The All Dorm Sauna. It must be a hundred degrees. She regretted not having worn a tank top and cut-offs instead of her Tri Beta angora sweater and summer-weight, wool skirt.

A huge jock stumbled off the dance floor, stomping her left foot.

"Ouch!" she cried.

"Sorry," he said. His partner came flying after him.

"Hey, Courtney!" said Winnie, grabbing hold of the jock's arm. "How's it going?"

"Hi," said Courtney, relieved to see a friendly face.

"You just missed KC," said Winnie. "She left before the dancing really got going." Winnie tugged her partner back onto the floor, disappearing in a swirl of bodies and clash of music.

Courtney folded her arms tightly. *I will have a good time,* she told herself. She winced at the music, at the distorted bass that rattled the huge speakers. No one else seemed to mind the terrible sound system. *Maybe you have to be eighteen years old and kooky to enjoy a party like this. No wonder KC left early. This is hardly the sort of evening that would excite someone with more mature interests.* A sharp, high-pitched electronic feedback cut through the noise in the room. Everyone pressed their hands to their ears until the piercing shriek died down.

Only the feel of Phoenix's strong arm calmed her. *So what if the speakers rattle and the pizza looks like plastic? What matters—all that matters—is that I'm with Phoenix.*

Phoenix slid her onto an old sofa. "Isn't this a great turnout?" he asked.

"Great," said Courtney, wiping tomato paste and crumbs off the cushion before she sat.

"I'll bet this is the most spirit this campus has seen in a long time. Hey, I forgot the drinks." He took another bite of pizza. "You thirsty?"

"Yes," Courtney answered.

"Be right back. Don't sell my pizza."

He headed for the punch bowls across the room, while Courtney looked around, trying again to get into the spirit of the party.

"Hey, good lookin'." A skinny guy in dirty jeans and wrinkled shirt stood over her. "Want company?"

"No, thank you," said Courtney. He sat down anyway. Courtney smelled beer on his breath.

"Someone is sitting there," she said.

He ignored her. "You one of the R.A.'s?" Stale cigarettes mixed with the beer smell. Did she look old enough to be an R.A.? Most of the Resident Advisors who watched over the dorm students were grad students in their mid-twenties. He leaned closer. "Which dorm are you in? I can come by later. Bring some brew."

"I'm not in a dorm. I'm not an R.A. And I'm saving that seat for my boyfriend." The word tasted strange. Boyfriend. Courtney liked the sound of it. Luckily, it had an effect on the tipsy Romeo.

"Sorry," he said, pushing up. "My mistake."

The music which had calmed down for a while picked up again. Courtney looked around the room, bored. That afternoon, she'd received a shipment of tapes from a friend at Yale. A Nobel Prize economist lectured there for three straight sessions and her friend had taped them all. Courtney couldn't wait to hear them. If Phoenix were the least little bit interested in finance, Courtney would have suggested they stay at her sorority, fix a batch of hot-air popcorn, and spend the night listening to the lectures. But he felt about finance the way she felt about pizza parties.

"Here you go." Phoenix handed her a small cup of punch.

"Thanks." Parched from the heat, Courtney gulped it down. Warm and sickeningly sweet, the punch left her thirstier than ever.

"Yo, Phoenix," said two ruddy-complexioned guys as they came up. "We're planning a rock climb in a couple of weeks with a local club that knows a spot about two hours from here. You interested?"

"Sure," said Phoenix.

"Great," said one of the guys. "We'll call when we have more info."

The other guy looked at Courtney before they left, as if trying to figure out if she was with Phoenix. Did she look that out of place with him?

"What was that about?" asked Courtney.

"I'm getting into rock climbing," said Phoenix.

"Oh. Is it like mountain climbing with those little picks and pitons?" she asked.

"No. You just walk right up the sheer side of a high rock, using these." He held up his bare hands. They were calloused and toughened from all his outdoor activities. Courtney pressed her soft and perfectly manicured hands against his. "I don't think these are the hands of a rock climber," he said, wrapping his strong fingers around hers.

The music stopped abruptly. One of the pizza servers climbed up onto the pizza table. His *Week at the U* T-shirt was smeared with tomato paste and assorted pizza toppings. "All right, everybody," he shouted, "It's time to limbo!"

"Limbo!" Students from all over the room shouted. "Limbo!" They ran to get line.

"Come on," said Phoenix, grabbing Courtney's hand and pulling her up off the sofa. "Let's limbo!"

"I'll watch," she said.

"Watching's no fun. Come on."

"No," she said, pulling away. "You go ahead. I'll wait back here."

His eyes clouded with disappointment. "Aren't you having fun?" he asked.

"Sure." She forced a smile. "I'm just a little hot in this sweater."

"Okay," he said, kissing her quickly, then dancing to the front of the line.

"Here I go," yelled Phoenix, checking to be sure she was watching. She smiled and he winked. The broom handle was only thigh-high.

"Limbo! Limbo! Limbo!" yelled the clapping crowd.

Phoenix stood in front of the broom handle, a look of mock fear on his face. The crowd laughed as he hiked up one pant leg, then the other, preparing to limbo under the pole.

Courtney clapped with the crowd but her heart wasn't in it. She needed to get out of this place. It wouldn't be right for her to drag Phoenix away though. He was just starting out in college, just beginning to have experiences. She mustn't take that away from him. She caught him as he danced around for another try under the broom.

"I've got a horrible headache," she shouted. "I think I'd better go home."

"I'll walk you," Phoenix shouted back.

"No, really. I won't be any fun. I'm just going to put a cold compress on my eyes and get some sleep."

"You're sure?" he said, the few remaining dancers already tugging him back into the line.

"Absolutely. Good luck on the limbo. I'll talk to you tomorrow."

Courtney backed slowly out of the crowd. She had told a little white lie. She didn't have a headache, but she would if she stayed one minute longer.

"Limbo! Limbo!" The chant of the crowd followed her out through the foyer and into the cool quiet evening air.

She did plan to lay down and rest. She would put her friend's tapes into the player and listen to three hours of economics lectures. Phoenix was enjoying the pizza party. She would enjoy her tapes. There was no reason she should feel the least bit guilty.

*   *   *

Derek had watched Kimberly all night. With all the work he had to do, all the projects he had to finish for physics class and *Week at the U,* he didn't have time to stand around having fun.

Now! he thought, not daring to take his eyes off her as he eased away from his friends. The limbo contest was going full force and he struggled through the mob. *Don't let her out of sight again.* Luckily, he was tall enough to see over the dancing heads. He kept Kimberly locked in view.

Usually he had so many things on his mind that he didn't focus on the people coming and going in his life. But Kimberly was different. Everything about her—bubbly personality, exciting mind, beautiful eyes, silky skin—had stopped him cold.

"Hi," he said, crowding into the space next to her.

Kimberly turned toward him, "Hi."

Was she happy to see him? He couldn't tell. "I see you've decrumbed yourself."

"I managed to find a vacuum."

Someone bumped into him from behind, pushing him into Kimberly. He pulled away quickly. "Sorry," he said.

"It is a little hectic around here."

The limbo contest ended and an easy rock song

came on. Derek looked down at his shoes, swallowing hard, getting up his courage.

"Want to dance?" he asked.

"With you?"

He stared at her. *Was she kidding him? Was she serious?* He couldn't read this girl. "That's what I had in mind."

Kimberly looked him over as if trying to decide.

"Well," he said, realizing he'd made a mistake, "if it's that rough a decision . . ."

"I just don't know," she said. "After that collision at the fencing demonstration, I'm not sure I can trust you not to knock me over again." Her beautiful mouth broke into a broad smile that lit up her face and Derek's heart all at the same time.

He held out his hand. "Sometimes you just have to take risks," he said.

Kimberly looked at his hand and slipped hers into it. They began dancing in small steps, their bodies close but not touching. At first he barely moved, waiting until they found one anothers' rhythm. He swayed easily from side to side and she followed. He moved forward and back, and she moved with him. They connected the way they had at the fencing exhibition, as if they were two halves of the same whole. Slowly, building with the music, he moved his arms and legs more wildly, letting go with the beat. She followed him, totally in sync, moving as if they were one.

The music changed to a slow song.

"Want to risk another one?" he asked.

"I guess I'm not maimed yet," she answered, laughing and checking her arms and legs.

"You sound disappointed."

She looked away. "Maybe I was hoping for a small injury. Just enough to get me out of *Week at the U*."

"Give me another chance," he teased. "I'll see what I can do."

"I guess I can live dangerously," she said, floating into his arms.

He held her close, loving the feel of her body, soft and warm, against his, her head nestled on his chest. He rested his cheek on her hair, inhaling the spicy smell of her.

The song ended much too soon, replaced almost immediately by a hard driving instrumental. Dancers all around them started jerking and jumping, bumping into them. Derek kept his arms around her, unwilling to let her go.

"How about going outside for some fresh air," he suggested.

"I'd like that," she said, swaying her body

against his. "Maybe if I'm lucky, I'll fall down the front stairs and sprain an ankle."

"Now, that's something worth seeing." He slipped his fingers through hers, keeping her close as they pushed through the dancers, out of Forest Hall, and onto the green.

The balmy, night air felt cool after the oppressive heat of the pizza party. Derek loved the feel of Kimberly's hand in his, her slender fragile fingers, her warm palm. *What else could be this important? What could matter more than walking hand in hand with Kimberly Dayton on a perfect, spring night? Nothing. Nothing at all. Not projects. Not homework. Not inhaling and exhaling. The world began and ended with the feel of her hand in his.*

They strolled along the green, past students sitting in small groups, Frisbee players, and other couples dotting the large, grassy area. He led her to an empty spot, spreading out his jacket for them to share, then lay back, his arms under his head. She settled in next to him, her fragrance settling over him like a gentle cloud. For a long time they lay together without talking.

Finally he turned his head, studying her exotic face with its cat's eyes and high cheekbones. *You are someone worth keeping, Kimberly Dayton. I won't louse up this time.* If he asked her out, and if she agreed to go out with him, he *wouldn't* forget to call her. He *wouldn't* forget to show up on time. He *wouldn't* do all the flaky things he did that loused up relationships. This would be different.

Her beautiful eyes studied the black sky crammed full of bright stars.

"There's Orion," said Derek, pointing to a formation of stars overhead. "And the Big Dipper."

"Where?"

"Over there. And a little to the left . . ." He showed her constellation after constellation.

"How do you know so much about astronomy?" asked Kimberly.

"I'd better," Derek said, turning on his side toward her. "I'm planning to be a science teacher."

Kimberly shook her head. "I didn't really believe you when you said that at the fencing exhibition," she said.

"Hey, don't sound so surprised. What's wrong with me being a teacher?"

"Nothing," said Kimberly. "I just don't hear too many people say they want to teach. It seems like everyone is studying to be in business or the arts."

"Like you?" asked Derek. "Are you planning to be a professional dancer?"

Kimberly flipped over on her stomach and

started pulling up blades of grass, piling them into a little mound.

Derek had to force himself not to reach out and rest his hand on her back, not to stroke her shoulders. He usually plunged into relationships at full speed. Kimberly didn't seem the type to rush. The last thing Derek wanted to do was scare her off. Not now. Not when he was just beginning to find out who she was, and what it was about her that made him want to spend every second around her.

"It's funny," Kimberly said. "Ever since I was a little girl, all I wanted to do was dance. The weird part is, I didn't ever want to be a professional dancer. I just loved moving to the music. I think if my mother wasn't the head of a dance company she would have left me alone. I mean, there are thousands of girls like me who love to dance. But do they have to become professionals?" She looked at Derek.

"You're asking me?" He lay down next to her, pulling up grass blades to add to her pile. "So what is it you want to do with your life?"

"That's just it, I don't know. Every time I turn around I fall in love with something else. I'm always going off in a million different directions at once."

"You sound like me," Derek said. He rolled on

his side, propping his head up on his hand, looking at Kimberly. He could watch her face all day and never get tired of it. Even more than her beauty, though, he loved her animation, her energy. "My father always says I'm a jack-of-all-trades, master of none. He's always after me to pick one thing and concentrate on it."

"So you picked science?"

"Science and kids."

"You're lucky," she said, stretching out next to him. "I wish I knew what I wanted. All I know is what I don't want. The more I'm forced to perform, the more I know I never want to be a professional dancer."

"Maybe you could teach dance."

"I don't know if I'd be any good as a teacher," she said. "Standing in front of a group of kids might be as scary as dancing in front of an audience."

"Are you kidding?" Derek sat up. "Kids are the best audience in the world. In fact . . ." he slowed, feeling an idea forming.

"What?"

"I think you just came up with the solution to my problem *and* yours."

"Derek." Kimberly sat up, smiling quizzically at him. "What are you talking about?"

"I've got this little problem." He took her hands in his without thinking. "I'm supposed to do a science demonstration for fourth and fifth graders. It's part of the education department's *Week at the U* program; Springfield kids are being bussed to the education building next Wednesday. But I still haven't come up with an idea that's going to make those kids as excited about science as I am."

Kimberly looked at him, trying to follow his rapid-fire babbling. "And just how do you see me fitting into this science demonstration of yours?" she asked.

"You can come and help me out."

"Like a magician's assistant?"

"Exactly! In fact, I'm thinking of using some basic magic tricks to demonstrate easy science principles."

"Derek Weldon," Kimberly widened her eyes in mock horror, "are you going to saw me in half?"

"What a great idea!" He pressed her hands between his, not wanting to let go, wondering if he was going to be able to hold onto someone so special. "Seriously," he said, "you'd be there to help me and keep me from lousing up. And you'll find out what it feels like to stand in front of a classroom. It might even take your mind off being nervous about your performance."

"I doubt that," she said. "Lately, it's all I think about."

A sudden wind shift brought a rush of cold air down from the mountains. "Brrrr," said Kimberly, shivering, rubbing her hands along her arms. Derek put his arms around her, holding her close. He could stay like this forever. Another blast of air sent the people on the green hurrying back into the dorms.

"Maybe we'd better go in," she said.

He helped her up, softly brushing a couple of leaves of grass out of her hair. He held her hand as he walked her back to Coleridge.

"So?" he said.

"I don't know," said Kimberly. "I'm so busy right now. When did you say the kids were coming?"

"Wednesday afternoon."

"Derek, my dance is Wednesday night."

"See?" he said, slipping his arm around her waist as they walked, his heart pounding so hard he couldn't believe she didn't hear it. "This is just what you need. You'll be so busy being sawed in half that you won't have time to get nervous about performing."

"And if your saw slips, I won't have to dance at all."

They laughed, stopping outside her dorm.

"So?" he said.

"I can't promise," said Kimberly. "But if I can possibly get my mind off my performance, I'll come help with your science demonstration."

"Fair enough," he said. "Two-thirty in the education building."

"Two-thirty. On Wednesday."

They stood silent for a moment. Derek longed to kiss Kimberly but what if she didn't want him to? He took a risk and bent to kiss her just as she turned away. He smashed into her nose.

"Owww," she said, rubbing the bridge. "I knew you were dangerous." Smiling, she kissed him quickly on the cheek and ran into her dorm.

"Dangerous," he said. Smiling, he turned back toward his dorm. "Dangerous." He laughed. "I'm dangerous!" he said, running down the green toward his dorm, jumping up to touch tree branches, hurdling a few couples still snuggling on the grass. He felt the warm touch of her lips on his cheek all the way home.

Thirteen

....

Faith was going to scream if Liza didn't stop talking. She hadn't shut up since they left their room, and now they were nearly at acting class.

"And Mr. Parcell, that was my high school drama coach who once understudied Brando on Broadway. Anyway, he taught us that . . ."

Faith barely listened to Liza's ramblings as they walked into the theater arts building. "Watch the tripods," warned a technician as they walked into the room. "Look out for the cables."

"Oh, no," Faith whispered. Bright lights were set up all over the classroom, and two cameras stood on either side of the portable stage. Thick cables ran from the equipment to wall outlets and technicians secured them to the floor with gaffer's tape. Christopher Hammond stood in front of the classroom dressed in his TV newscaster blazer.

"Can we have five students in these front seats?" asked Christopher. Faith stepped back, slinking into the shadows. Liza practically knocked her over running up to the front.

"Okay, class," said Mr. Francosi as he held up his hands for quiet. "Try and forget the cameras." The class laughed. "I know, I know. How do you ignore a raging bull charging right at you? But you have to try. Play to the audience. Play to the windows. Play to the desk. Whatever will help you get into the role. Mr. Minkus, will you start us off please."

The short, intense southerner grabbed a stool and stepped up on the stage. He turned his back on the audience, his shoulders heaving as he took a few deep breaths. When he turned, his entire face had changed. He looked off stage left and began talking to some imaginary person. "And if I can ever be of help to you again," he said a few minutes later, finishing the reading, "don't hesitate to call. You know I'll be waiting." He winked, waved at the imaginary person, then jumped off the stool and walked away. The class broke into applause as he returned. Bowing deeply, he grabbed the stool and bounded off the stage.

"All right," said Mr. Francosi. Faith jumped. Francosi was standing directly behind her chair. "What was Mr. Minkus's objective?"

"To be friendly," said the class.

"To befriend," said Francosi. "Nice job."

Minkus grunted. He'd turned back into his old, solemn self again.

Faith held her breath. She could feel Francosi's eyes scanning the room. She just knew he was going to put his hand on her shoulder and make her do her reading next. *Please not me, please not me, please not me,* she thought with all her might. Christopher stood to one side of the stage, his shifty eyes looking out at the class. A nervous chill ran through her. Why did he still have the power to upset her? *Please please please not me!*

"Who would like to go next?" asked Francosi.

"Me!" shouted Liza, jumping up onto the stage. Faith blew out a sigh of relief, grateful for once that her roommate was such a ham.

"Hey, gorgeous, you got those cameras primed and ready?" called Liza, squinting against the bright lights.

"Ready when you are," said Christopher.

"How'd ya know I was talkin' to you?" she said, winking boldly. The class laughed.

"All right, hold onto your wigs," Liza said, "herrrrrre we go."

She walked to the edge of the stage, hopped down, and left the room. Students broke out in surprised laughter. Suddenly, Liza burst back into the room, arms stretched out wide, head thrown back, a huge smile on her face as she jumped up onto the stage singing. "I'm so ga-LAAAAaaaaAAAAaaaaAAAAd you're here."

Faith joined in the laughter as Liza pranced up and back, working the crowd, mugging for the camera, bugging out her eyes, frizzing out her hair, blowing bubbles from a huge bubble jar hanging from a string around her neck.

"And if I can EVer EVer EVer be of the least teensiest weensiest help to you again," she said, comically wiggling both eyebrows up and down, "don't hesi*tate* to call." She wrinkled her nose and squealed. The class roared. " 'Cause, you just know I'll be waiting." She hunched over, walking like Groucho Marx smoking a cigar, and walked right off stage.

"Encore," someone called. Someone else whistled. The applause went on and on as Liza took several bows. "Encore!"

"Not today," said Francosi, standing right next to Faith. Maybe he was too close to see her. Maybe he'd focus on the front of the class. She checked her watch. There was still a lot of class time left. "All right, what was Miss Ruff's objective?"

"To crack us up?" someone asked.

"If you mean to amuse," said Francosi, "I think you hit that right on the laugh button. Well done, Miss Ruff." Liza bowed again, winking at the camera before she sat back down.

"Miss Crowley?"

"Y . . . yes?"

Francosi drummed his fingers on her desk. "Would you share your reading with us?"

"Y . . . yes," she squeaked, swallowing. Her throat felt like it was lined with sandpaper. All the moisture in her mouth dried up.

Faith walked to the front of the room, carefully stepping over the crisscross of cables. *This will all be over in five more minutes,* she told herself. *Just five minutes of your life. That's all. So what if you're about as sexy as a loaf of white bread? So what if the camera is going to capture your performance on film for the rest of recorded history? Just five minutes. Then you can go home and hide until you're old and gray and no one remembers what a fool you made of yourself.*

She stepped up on the stage trying to remember the first words of the reading.

"Take a minute to get settled," said Francosi.

"Thanks," she said.

She turned her back on the class to compose herself. Taking a deep breath through her nose, she let it out slowly through her mouth. She could feel Christopher's eyes on her, like two knives in her back. There was nothing she wanted more than to put him in his place. He probably still thought she was that same naive freshman he'd taken advantage of when she'd first arrived at U. of S.

"Hey, roomie," said Liza. "You only practiced this five thousand million times. Remember? I'm so glad you're here."

A gift! Liza meant to be funny, but she'd thrown Faith a lifeline. Faith turned. One of the bright camera lights flickered, flashing her shadow against the wall.

"Hold it," said a technician. "I have a loose connection. One minute."

A reprieve. In front of her, Christopher worked with the lighting guy to fix the problem. She'd been in awe of Christopher those first weeks on campus, but now she knew he wasn't worthy of admiration. He was just a ruthless user of people.

And there was no way she'd allow Christopher or anyone else to use her again.

"That should do it," said Christopher.

Faith felt the intense heat as the lamp flared up.

"That's good," said Christopher, backing into the shadows beyond the lights. "Ready."

Faith looked up slowly. The lights were so bright she couldn't see anyone in the audience. In a way, it was like being alone. The way she'd been when she practiced in her bedroom.

"All right, Miss Crowley," said Francosi. "Any time."

Walking to the edge of the stage, Faith slid one hand down her thigh. "I'm so glad you're here," she said, her husky voice barely a whisper, her eyes fixed to a spot to the left of the light. "For a while," she untied the ribbon on the end of her braid, "I was afraid you weren't coming."

Slowly working the braid open, she talked to the imaginary lover. She swam into the reading, loving the hush that had settled over the class. Little by little she undid her braid until, near the end, she took out the last twist, shaking a cascade of silky hair as she said,

"And if I can *ever* be of help to you again," she pressed a finger to her lips, then blew the kiss toward the light, "don't hesitate to call." She turned and did a Marilyn Monroe walk to the back of the stage, pausing a moment to turn back to the audience. "You *know* I'll be waiting."

And then she was off the stage, out the door and into the hall.

Yes! Yes! Yes! She pressed her hand over her mouth, not believing what she'd just done. *Who was that person on stage?* she thought. Not her. Not Faith Crowley. But someone. Some part of her. Yes. The performance was good and she knew it.

Lifting her head, setting her shoulders back, she walked back into the room, beaming at the applause and loud whistles. Without looking at Christopher, she sensed him staring at her. She felt a shift of power. Now he was interested in her and she was the one in control. What a great feeling!

"That was some performance, Miss Crowley," said Mr. Francosi.

"Thanks," said Faith, breathless, shaking as she returned to her chair. Where had she ever found the nerve?

"All right," said Francosi. "And what was Miss Crowley's objective in that scene?"

"To turn us on?" said a guy up front.

"And did she ever," said someone else.

Faith felt her cheeks burn as the class laughed.

Thank goodness the back of the room was dark. No one could see how red her face must be.

"To seduce," said Francosi. "Yes. Very good, Miss Crowley. Very, very, convincing."

After two more readings, the class ended. Faith grabbed her books and headed for the door.

"Not bad, Crowley," said Christopher, following her out into the hall. "Looks like you've got some real talent."

"Gee, Hammond," she said, "how nice of you to notice."

"Hi, Christopher," said Liza, pushing out of the classroom.

Christopher ignored her. His eyes were locked on Faith's.

"Not only did I notice, Faith, but I plan to spotlight your performance on tonight's show." He lifted the right half of his mouth slightly. Faith remembered that look. It was meant to seduce. The effect it had on her now was to nauseate. She felt Liza moving around, trying to get in on the discussion. Christopher moved closer to Faith, their bodies nearly touching.

"What's it going to cost me to have you make me famous?" she asked, sweetly.

"No one buys their way onto my show," he said. He lifted a strand of her long hair, running a thumb down her neck. "My show's successful because I know good talent when I see it. I know how to show people off in their best light."

"Sure you do, Christopher." She lifted his hand off her neck and dropped it. "But I doubt you let anyone's light outshine yours."

A confused look crossed his eyes, like the hunter whose prey escapes. Faith lifted her mouth in a little half-smile, turned on her heel, and made her exit.

Curtain, she thought. *The End. Applause. Applause.*

Fourteen

KC practically skipped along the street on her way to Springfield Faces. She was going to show them just who was smarter. Smiling, she leap-frogged a fire hydrant and turned onto Fifth Street.

She hummed to herself all the way to The Strand, Springfield's exclusive shopping area. But KC wasn't dressed to the nines today. She hadn't borrowed a fancy cashmere sweater from Lauren, and she hadn't brought her expensive briefcase or worn high heel pumps. And she certainly hadn't stayed up all night worrying about her makeup and hair. It was almost fun to stroll along in an old pair of Winnie's torn jeans, one of Peter's stretched out T-shirts and her own gym shoes with the laces pulled out.

"You should try wearing more comfortable clothes," Peter had said a few times. "You're always so dressed up." Peter should see her now. Too bad he was on assignment, covering a *Week at the U* 10K run for the campus paper.

KC passed her favorite window-shopping stores. For once she didn't even bother looking at the elegant displays. Her mind was focused on what she would do when she got to Springfield Faces.

"I am Kahia Cayanne," she would say, in all her ragtag glory. The staff would try to hurry her out. KC could just picture the office, filled with young hopefuls, all dressed up the way KC had dressed for her Adela Loomis interview, but KC would stand firm.

"You may be able to con some people into thinking you're a modeling agency," she'd say, loud enough for the other girls to hear and be warned. "But I am a business major. And I know a bait-and-switch when I see it. You say you'll make us models, then *you* charge *us* for modeling lessons. No, I don't want to sign up for modeling lessons. I don't want to join your charm school. The only reason I'm here is to get my photos back." Then she'd thrust out her hand, take her photos, and leave.

Look out, all you fine young crooks, she thought, turning into the Lorimax building. *KC Angeletti is on her way.*

KC walked right through the double glass doors and took the elevator up to Springfield Faces.

A frazzled brunette in jeans and a blousy shirt, with pencils sticking out of her frizzy hair, sat behind the desk. KC couldn't believe how disheveled she looked. At least Adela Loomis made an effort to look professional. The woman was trying to answer the ringing phones but seemed to keep disconnecting people. KC saw the manila envelope with her photos in a large pile behind the woman. Maybe KC should just grab the photos and leave.

But before KC could take action, the woman reached out and touched her arm. "KC Angeletti! I can't believe I didn't recognize you," she said, ignoring the phones. "Well, yes I can, since I didn't have my glasses on. Sit down, sit down. She held out her hand.

Stunned, KC shook it. This wasn't at all what she expected.

"My name is Beth Diane," the woman continued. "Actually, it's Dinahmolsky, but that was too hard for everyone to deal with so I've shortened it here at work." Beth Diane pulled KC's file out of the pack and emptied the contents onto the desk. "I see you've also shortened your name. Although, Kahia Cayanne is quite lovely. Lyrical. But KC is cute and upbeat. 'Of course, whatever you want to use is fine with us."

Use? Fine with us? KC was confused. This woman didn't sound anything like Adela Loomis. Was it possible she actually wanted KC to model?

"I've been looking forward to this meeting. Your photos are wonderful. I've never heard of your photographer—"

"Peter Dvorsky," said KC.

"Yes. His work is certainly outstanding. You have so many different looks that I think we'll be able to get you as much work as you're willing to take."

What was she talking about? Couldn't she see the way KC looked? Didn't she understand KC had dressed this way as an insult, as a joke?

"Any questions?" asked Beth Diane.

KC thought about the $300 Adela Loomis had demanded before she'd try and get KC work.

"How much do you charge to find me jobs?" asked KC.

"Charge? Oh, you mean our fee."

Here it comes, thought KC.

"We don't charge you anything. What happens is, we call you whenever someone is looking for your type. We can send you out strictly as a model or, if you like, we can send you on acting auditions —commercials, documentaries, that sort of thing. There's all sorts of work around. Then, if you audition and get the job, our agency takes ten percent of what you earn."

"Can you tell me how much your models earn?" KC asked.

"Well, it depends on the work of course. Our runway models usually earn around $60 to $80 an hour."

A tingle ran up KC's back. Was it possible she could earn money like that?

"If you have a speaking part in a T.V. commercial, you earn money each time it's shown. That can add up to hundreds or thousands of dollars depending on whether it's a local or national spot."

KC's head swam. With money like that, she could stop worrying about paying for school and the sorority, and all the other money problems that sometimes kept her up at night.

"Any other questions?" Beth Diane smiled and KC's instincts told her this was a person she could trust.

Later, as KC got ready to leave, Beth Diane handed her a business card. "I have an interesting audition coming up next week," she said. "I think you're exactly the type they're looking for. Call me tomorrow if you decide anything." KC took the card and put it carefully in her pocket.

"Thanks," she said, "for everything. I'll get back to you by tomorrow."

KC walked to the elevator, waiting as calmly as she could until it came. Stepping inside the empty car, she waited until the doors slid closed, then jumped up, screaming, "Yes! Yes! Yes! Eeeeaaaaah-hhaaaa!!!!" She stopped as the doors opened, but judging from the startled faces of two women waiting to get on, her voice had carried down the elevator shaft and into the lobby.

She couldn't wait. She had to tell *someone*. KC fed coins into the lobby phone. Who should she call first? Peter was in class. Besides, she wanted to tell him in person how much Beth Diane loved his photos. She tried to remember Faith and Winnie's schedules. She dialed Faith.

"They're really a modeling agency," she said. "And they want me!"

"Wait," said Faith, "I'll put this on conference with Winnie." KC held the phone, waiting as Faith dialed Winnie, looking at herself in the lobby mirrors. They didn't reflect an ugly girl in torn clothes. What KC saw was someone so happy, all the joy shone right through, casting a rosy glow on her cheeks, a merry twinkle in her eyes.

Winnie answered the phone and the three friends laughed and screamed.

"We've got to celebrate!" said Winnie.

"Let's meet at five in the dining commons," said Faith. "They're going to show *Week at the U* coverage on the big screen TV."

"It's a date," said KC, hanging up, still too happy to think straight. She dug out more money and called Courtney. "I owe everything to you," said KC. "I never would have thought of modeling to earn money. You're a real friend. Thanks."

Fifteen

·····················

Courtney hung up the phone and curled back up on her bed.

"At least someone's happy," she groaned.

Outside her closed door, Tri Betas ran through the halls, laughing, yelling, getting ready for the last day of *Week at the U* events. The girls had decided to serenade every fraternity house on Greek Row and were excitedly picking out songs to sing, making up matching outfits to wear.

"Courtney?" The muffled voice was followed by three short knocks on her door. "You in?"

"Come on in, Diane." Diane Woo popped her

head in. "Sure you don't want to come sing with us?"

"Sure. I'm feeling sort of draggy."

"Okay. Yodel if you change your mind." She closed the door after her.

Courtney opened her statistics book for the fifth time, forcing herself to focus on the charts, graphs, and intricate timetables. Phoenix's face, with his clear, honest eyes, his trusting, loving face, floated up off the page. Phoenix, and Phoenix, and Phoenix. Courtney slammed the book shut.

"What am I going to do?" she asked out loud. "Tonight is going to be a disaster. Why am I making Phoenix go see Kimberly perform. He hated the international economics lecture as much as I loathed the pizza party. How can two people who like each other so much, have such totally different likes and dislikes?"

A few more Tri Betas joined the group outside. They started tying bows around the candles, preparing for the serenade. Courtney didn't feel like doing anything lately. Her energy was gone. She had trouble falling asleep, and when she finally did, she was restless, waking up on and off all night.

She slid open her desk drawer, lifting out the

photos Marielle Danner had taken of her and Phoenix swimming in their underwear at Hosmer Lake. Marielle had wanted to destroy Courtney after Courtney had kicked her out of Tri Beta. She thought the photographs would shock Greek Row and that Courtney would be forced to step down as president. But instead, the photographs had boosted Beta Beta Beta's image.

"That was such a special day," Courtney said, remembering Hosmer Lake. It had been a hot day during sorority rush week. Courtney, still recuperating from hitting her head against a pier, had ducked out of rush activities to be with Phoenix. They had picnicked on shore, then, on the spur of the moment, Phoenix had stripped down to his underwear and jumped into the cool lake. Courtney, doing the first truly spontaneous thing of her life, stripped down to her lacy bra and panties and dove right in after him.

"It was such fun," she said wistfully. "To do what I wanted to do exactly when I wanted to do it, without thinking it through, worrying it to death, squeezing all the life out of the idea."

Courtney put the photos back in the drawer and pushed it closed. Phoenix had helped her through that difficult rush week. He showed her the soft and loving side of herself, helped her become a more caring leader to the girls of Tri Beta. She owed him so very much. How could she hurt him, and herself, by breaking up?

"What to do?" She frowned at the knock on her door. "Come in," she said expecting it to be one of the girls wanting to borrow something to wear for the serenade. She tried to gear up to be friendly, although she wasn't feeling very social just now.

The door opened and Phoenix walked in.

"Phoenix?" said Courtney. He stood in the doorway, awkward, uncomfortable. *What was he doing here?* Girls running through the halls looked at him curiously as they passed. Courtney wasn't in the habit of entertaining guys in her room. "Come in, come in," she said.

He walked in and closed the door behind him. "Hi," he said, running a hand through his long hair. "I . . . um," he cleared his throat.

"Sit down," said Courtney.

"No . . . I'm not staying . . . I just . . . that is . . ." He shifted from foot to foot. Dressed in hiking shorts and an old T-shirt, he looked like an ad for a nature magazine.

Courtney felt more torn than ever. Part of her wanted to run to him, hold him, forget the rest of the world existed. The other part told her they were not right for each other. How could she possibly hurt someone so honest, so open?

"That is," he said, "I . . . needed to talk to you."

"Is something wrong?" she asked softly.

"Well, it's just that . . . it's so beautiful outside . . ."

"Yes?"

"And, well, it doesn't seem like tonight will be a night I'll be wanting to spend indoors. I mean, sitting in a dance concert."

Courtney searched his eyes and saw the hurt and the sadness. She saw that Phoenix had been feeling some of the same things she had. Suddenly the weight on her heart lifted.

"And I thought," he said, "that is, I want, well, when I stopped and thought about what I really want to do tonight—"

"Yes?"

". . . what I *really* want to do is to go on a night hike in the hills."

"I understand," said Courtney.

His eyes widened in surprise and relief. "You do? You really do?"

"I do," she said. "Come over here." She patted the bed next to her. Phoenix sat down, leaning back against the wall. She took his hand, tracing the veins along the back with her fingers. "I've been sitting here wondering what to say to you. You mean so much to me. You've added so much to my life."

"That works both ways, Courtney."

"I know. That's why it hurts so much to know we're not working out. We're not a couple. I'm relieved you made the first move. You're a much stronger person than I am."

"Hey, come on, I'm not—"

"Yes, you are. And I'm grateful." Courtney smoothed her soft skin over his callouses. "I know how much you hated the economics lecture."

"It showed, huh?"

"Yes." She smiled at his ruddy face, his boyish eyes. "It showed. Oh, don't you see, you couldn't hide your true feelings if you wanted to, Phoenix Cates. You are the most honest person I've ever met."

His face reddened and he looked down at their hands. "I know you didn't have fun at the pizza party. I should have left when you did, and walked you home."

"No. I really didn't want you to. You were having fun. That's our problem. We don't have fun doing the same things."

"That's sort of the way I have it figured," he

said. He squeezed her hand, a tear in the corner of his eye. None of the men Courtney knew showed emotion. She would probably never find anyone like Phoenix again.

"I love you, Phoenix," she said, "in a very special way. But we aren't right for each other."

He nodded, swallowing hard. "I guess I'd better go." He slid off the bed, his lanky body awkward in her frilly room. Courtney got up and put her arms around his neck.

"Thank you," she said, kissing him on the cheek, "for everything." He smiled and hugged her tight.

"Thanks for understanding," he said. "I hope you'll still be my friend."

"Just you try and stop me," she said. Then he was gone and Courtney stared out the empty doorway. She felt a small, empty space in her heart that Phoenix used to fill, but, even more, she felt a peaceful calm that told her she'd done the right thing. It was time to get on with her life and look to her future.

A group of sisters raced by. "Come on, Courtney," said Diane, grabbing Courtney's hand, pulling her down the hallway. "I know you don't want to, but we need your voice to drown out my monotone."

Courtney laughed, letting her friend draw her into the craziness of the serenade. There was nothing wrong with spur-of-the-moment action. It felt good to plunge into things without thinking them to death first. That was true whether it was a romance with Phoenix or a swim in a lake or a serenade of fraternity houses.

Her life would go on, a more caring, spontaneous, and honest life, thanks to the influence of Phoenix Cates. Courtney ran out onto the street, her strong voice joining the "Tri Beta's All" song, as she linked arms with her sisters and marched happily down the block.

Sixteen

•••••••••••••••••••••••••••

"**K**imberly Anne Dayton," Kimberly said under her breath, "I think you have finally gone off the deep end."

She'd rushed from her interpretive dance class to the education building, arriving just as three huge busloads of school children disappeared inside. What was she doing here? It was 2:20 Wednesday afternoon. Her dance performance was less than seven hours away. Was she practicing? Was she warming up? Was she doing one single thing she should have been doing to prepare? No, she was not. She'd run over—not even stopping to change clothes—to help Derek demonstrate science to a bunch of grade school kids.

Kimberly slung her dance bag over her shoulder, tightened her wrap skirt around her leotard, and followed the last line of students into the building.

"May I help you?" asked a woman with a clipboard stationed at the base of the stairs.

"Yes, I'm looking for Derek Weldon. He's giving a science program to fourth and fifth graders."

"I'll check," said the woman, running a finger down a long list.

Young voices echoed through the old brick building. Footsteps stomped up the staircase. The sounds threw Kimberly back into her own past. She'd forgotten what it felt like to be this young. She could almost smell white paste and cafeteria food.

"Here it is," said the woman. "Derek Weldon, science demonstration. That would be room 305. Take the yellow line to the west stairwell, then up to three."

Kimberly followed the yellow stripe painted on the floor. She shouldn't be here. She needed to polish a few sections of her performance. Her stomach churned. She could walk out right now. After all, she hadn't promised Derek she would come. She only said she'd come and help out if she could. Then she remembered Saturday night, all cuddled up next to Derek on the green, listening to his excitement about teaching, and about having her be his assistant. Maybe Derek was right. Maybe helping him out would take her mind off tonight's performance.

The stairway walls to the third floor were covered with paper tulips cut out of construction paper, stories written on wide-lined paper, and poems brightly illustrated by their young authors. The education building reminded Kimberly of her own grade school. She'd loved it, loved her teachers, the classes, the excitement of having the whole world opened up to her. No wonder Derek wanted to teach. How could she have forgotten the magic?

"Are you a dancer?" The skinny girl getting a drink at the fountain startled Kimberly.

"W . . . why, yes," said Kimberly. "At least, sometimes. How did you know?"

"You're dressed like dancers on TV."

"Ah," said Kimberly. The girl, all skinny arms and legs, knobby elbows and knees, reminded Kimberly of herself at that age. "What grade are you in?" she asked.

"Fourth."

"I'll bet you're here for the science class."

The girl nodded. "I hate science," she said, making a face. "It's boring." They walked down the hall towards room 305.

"Science won't be boring today," said Kimberly.

"How do you know?"

"Because I'm helping the teacher in that class." Why did she say that? Now she'd have to stay and help Derek.

"Really?" The girl's eyes widened. "Can you teach us to dance, too? I like to dance."

"Me?" Kimberly laughed. "I don't think I'm much of a teacher."

"I know a few steps," said the girl, spinning suddenly down the empty hall.

It reminded Kimberly of the series of dramatic spins she'd choreographed at the end of "Magician at Midnight." Cape flying, music building, Kimberly would stretch her long legs into a series of dramatic leaps, then spin back across the stage on a diagonal. It was one of the sections she wanted to work on before tonight's performance. Her stomach churned again. She felt the beginnings of nervous cramps.

The girl twirled, her feet too far apart, her head spinning around and around.

"You'll get dizzy that way," said Kimberly. "Here, let me show you how to spot."

"Spot?"

"Yes. It's a dancer's secret. You pick a spot on a wall the same height as your eyes."

"Like that yellow tulip?"

"Perfect," said Kimberly. "Now, slowly start to turn around, keeping your eyes glued to that tulip as long as you can." The girl turned slowly. "Now, when you absolutely have to turn your head, snap it around so you see the flower again." She watched the girl try it a few times. "Good," said Kimberly. The young dancer beamed. "That's it. Excellent."

"This is hard."

"Only at first. If you practice at home you'll see how much better you can spin." Kimberly felt a warm glow inside. Maybe she did know a thing or two she could teach, after all.

"This is it," said the girl, stopping at a classroom door. The room was jammed with students, but Derek wasn't inside. It was only 2:29. She'd wait in the hall until he came.

The girl grabbed Kimberly's hand. "Come on," she said, pulling Kimberly into the noisy room.

"Oh, good," said the teacher. "You've come to do the science demonstration."

"Well, actually, I'm assisting. Derek should be here—"

"And your name is? . . ."

"Kimberly. Kimberly Dayton. But I'm just—"

"Children." The teacher clapped her hands. "Children, your attention please. Miss Dayton will be teaching you science this afternoon." She gathered up her purse and keys. "I'm just going to run to a few of the other classes to make sure they're set up all right. I'll be back later."

"But—" Kimberly watched in disbelief as the teacher walked out of the room. When she turned toward the class, thirty pairs of eyes stared at her, waiting.

Derek, where are you?! I can't do this. She turned to leave, to get the teacher back. Her little friend sat in the last seat. The girl's wide eyes stared up at Kimberly with such hope, such admiration. . . . *I promised her this class would be fun. I promised to make science special.* The girl crossed her skinny arms on her desk, waiting. *Am I always going to run out when things get rough?* The girl smiled. Kimberly smiled back.

Straightening her back, lifting her chin, Kimberly walked as regally as she could to the front of the room. Stalling for time, she picked up a piece of chalk and began to write Miss Dayton on the board. The chalk screeched on the downstroke of the "D."

"Eeeiiiiiii!" cried the class, slapping their hands over their ears. Kimberly kept writing. The chalked snapped in half as she crossed the "t." The broken piece flew across the board, hit the chalk ledge, and plopped into an aquarium. The class howled.

Kimberly turned around. Some children were standing in their seats, while others were flopping over the arm rests. If she didn't do something immediately, they would be tearing up the room by the time Derek came—if he even bothered to show up.

"Perfect!" she said, clapping her hands, smiling. The class stopped, looking at her quizzically. *Please let this work,* she thought. "You have just done physics."

"What?" said the students, sliding back into their seats. "What's that?" Kimberly wrote ACTION on the left side of the board and REACTION on the right.

"I screeched the chalk, you covered your ears. Right?"

"Right," shouted the class. Kimberly wrote "Chalk Screech" under ACTION, and "Cover Ears" under REACTION.

"Then," she said, "the chalk flew into the aquarium, and you laughed. Right?"

"Right," they said, laughing again.

She wrote "Chalk in Fish Bowl" under ACTION and "Laughter" under REACTION. She smiled, doubting this free-form physics was exactly what Professor Jobst had in mind. No matter. First, she'd get the children's attention, then she'd worry about teaching them.

"There is a kind of math called physics," she said, writing the word on the board. "Part of physics says that for every action," she tapped the word on the board, "there is an equal and opposite reaction. We see physics every day, all around us."

"I don't," said a tough looking girl. A couple of her friends sniggered.

"Has anyone ever pushed you on a swing?" asked Kimberly.

"Yeah. So?"

"What about the rest of you?" All the hands went up. "Well, physics teaches us that something can't be pushed unless something else is pushing."

"I know *that,*" said the tough girl.

"We all know that," said Kimberly, gently. "Which is why physics is so interesting to study. Physics is the science that tries to explain ordinary things we see every day."

"Like what?"

Kimberly thought for a moment. "Has anyone here ever seen a leaf fall from a tree?" she asked next. All the hands went up. "Has any one here ever thrown a ball into the air and watched it come back down?" All the hands went up again. She had them now. All the eyes were watching her, waiting, demanding to be informed, interested, involved. The trick was to keep their attention.

"Watch this," said Kimberly. She walked to one side of the room, and taking a short, three-step approach, took a long leap across the front of the classroom.

"Wow!"

"Did you see that?"

"Watch again," said Kimberly. "This time I'll keep on going up until I reach the ceiling." She leapt again, her long legs carrying her easily across the room. She landed softly on the other side.

"Neat."

"Awesome!"

"Darn," said Kimberly, pretending to pout. "Why did I come back down? Why didn't I just keep going up and up and up?" The class was silent. "I want to fly. Why can't I?"

"Because you're not Supergirl." The class laughed.

"Right," said Kimberly, laughing with them. "But why else can't I fly?"

"Gravity?" asked a girl.

"Right." Kimberly wrote it on the board. "Over 300 years ago, a famous scientist named Isaac Newton," she said, writing the name on the board, "wondered why things fell."

"I know about Isaac Newton," said a boy. "He was in a comic book, sitting under a tree. An apple fell on his head and knocked him out." The children laughed some more.

"I don't know about the apple knocking him out," said Kimberly, "but that's the guy. Now, Isaac Newton—"

She walked up and down the rows, smiling at the bright young faces, not at all nervous about being "on stage" in the classroom. She'd just breezed through the same leap she was terrified of doing in tonight's performance. It was as if her body was free to move when her mind wasn't focused on dance. Tunnel vision, her mother called it. It was what a great dancer had to have. A life of dance and only dance. Kimberly needed more. She needed to widen her world, stop shutting out other parts of herself. Her most creative movement began as soon as she let the nondancer in her come out.

"—and called them Newton's Three Laws of Motion," she said. "That's what makes a scientist. Someone who looks at things, wonders why they happen, then tries to figure it all out." Kimberly could almost hear all those young minds soaking up the ideas and information. She was more than just a dancer. She had things to offer besides leaps and spins.

"Hi, boys and girls," said Derek, rushing into the classroom, his arms loaded down with books, papers, and bags. He'd worn Mickey Mouse suspenders for the occasion, and a T-shirt imprinted with a large photo of Albert Einstein. "Sorry I'm late!" he said, trying to sound cheerful. Kimberly saw how nervous he was.

"This is your science teacher today," said Kimberly, "Mr. Derek Weldon." She helped Derek carry his things up front.

"Here," he said, handing a kid a large bag of balloons. "Pass these out. Everyone, please take a balloon and blow it up. But don't tie the end. We're going to do an experiment." Kids called out for balloons, talking, shouting.

"Where have you *been?*" Kimberly whispered.

"My experiment in chem lab exploded," he said,

pulling jars and rubber bands out of his bag. "I figured you could hold down the fort."

"I am going to hold down your head—preferably under water—if you ever flake out on me like this again."

"It's not my fault—"

"It's never your fault."

"But I—"

"But nothing." She reached over and snapped one of his suspenders. "You listen up, Derek Weldon. If you and I are going to have any kind of relationship—"

"Relationship?" His eyes widened behind his wire rim glasses.

"—you are going to have to stop trying to do a thousand things at one time."

"Relationship?" A balloon whizzed past them, splatting against the chalk board.

"Sorry," said the student chasing it. "It got away." Other students started letting their balloons go, chasing them all over the classroom.

"I got all these future scientists here started," said Kimberly, hoisting her dance bag back on her shoulder.

"I can see that—"

"I think you'd better take over. I have some

things of my own to take care of for tonight's performance."

"You're leaving me alone?"

"Toughen up, Weldon. It's only a room full of kids." A balloon zapped him in the head. "And remember, I expect to see you in the audience, eight o'clock sharp."

"I'll try to—"

"Don't *try*. Be there." She shook a fist at him. "Or you're going to experience Kimberly Dayton's personal law of action-reaction first hand."

Seventeen

··

Winnie ducked under the wall-mounted dining commons TV and flopped down on the old sofa next to Faith and KC. Her green neon shorts clashed with the peach colored sofa, but Winnie was in a clashing kind of mood. She slipped off her boots and curled her legs, clad in striped tights up under her.

"You okay?" asked Faith, rolling up the bottoms of her OshKosh overalls.

"Fine," said Winnie. "If you don't count the fact that my entire life is falling apart."

"That's a relief," said KC, winking at Faith. "We were afraid it might be something serious."

The commons foyer filled with other students waiting to go in to dinner. A couple of engineering students tinkered with the back of the TV, trying to get KRUS to come in more clearly.

"Let's make a Winnie sandwich!" said Faith. She and KC pushed together, squeezing Winnie between them.

"I give! I give!" cried Winnie.

"Are you going to stop being such a blah?" asked KC.

"Such a yuck?" asked Faith.

"Yes! Yes! I swear!"

They eased up. "Tell old Auntie KC what's the matter," said KC.

"Everyone's life is great except mine," said Winnie, pulling on her tights. "You're all doing such great things. KC's going to work as a real live model, become world-famous, and live in a villa in Paris."

"I certainly hope so," said KC. She licked the tip of a finger and smoothed it over her eyebrow. "Of course, I'll invite you for caviar and champagne."

"What about me?" asked Faith.

"That's easy," Winnie said. "You're going to direct the world's top money-making movies and hobnob with all the great stars."

"Sounds great," said Faith. "But don't think I'm going to forget all you little people who made it all possible."

"Go ahead. Make fun. But what have I done? Nothing, that's what."

The students cheered as the picture on the TV went from fuzzy to clear. The engineering students bowed. "Now," they said, "we'll try for some color besides purple."

"Think Winnie-the-Pooh's feeling a little sorry for herself?" asked KC.

"Her life is a wasteland," said Faith. "She never does anything."

"Except answer phones at the Hotline," added KC.

"Big deal," said Winnie. She kept pulling on her tights.

"It is a big deal," said KC. "Not everyone can help people with problems."

"But I want to do something important, something great, something that will make people sit up and take notice."

"Color!" said the engineers. The crowd applauded and whistled. A few people tossed pennies which the engineers happily scooped up.

Since her fight with Josh, Winnie hadn't felt like studying and she'd barely run or worked out. The few times she'd seen Josh, he'd pretended to be with some other girl so Winnie grabbed the nearest guy and pretended to be with him. It was awful!

What was it Travis used to sing when they argued? "When love goes wrong, nothing goes right." She used to tell Travis it was a dumb song. Now she knew better.

"It's starting!" Everyone in the room turned toward the TV.

"Turn the sound up."

"Down in front."

"Dim the lights so we can see better."

The theme music for the five o'clock news came on. After the world news and local headlines, Christopher's Hammond's *Week at the U* coverage began.

"There's Kimberly," said Faith. They watched Kimberly go through the motions of her dance.

"She's a much better dancer than that," said Winnie.

"I told you Christopher the Insensitive came barging into her class when she wasn't ready."

"Thank goodness she's not here to see it," said

KC. "It would make her even more nervous about tonight's performance."

Next, a clip of the All Dorm Pizza Party came on. A cheer went up as Christopher's crew did a close-up shot on the burnt pizza, the toilet paper decorations, then zoomed in on students dancing to a wild song.

"There I am," shouted a girl.

"I look weird when I dance," said a jock.

"You always look weird," laughed his friend.

Then Josh came on the screen, his arms and legs flying. Winnie's heart raced.

"Hey, Josh, that's you," someone yelled.

Winnie looked around. Josh stood right behind her, staring at her. Winnie's world screeched to a stop. How long had he been there? She wanted to reach up and touch him so badly, she ached.

He quickly looked away, embarrassed that she'd caught him watching her. She looked away, too. But Winnie had seen the look in his eyes, the hurt and the longing. Was he feeling as miserable as she was? She looked back but he was gone.

"Oh, no," Faith groaned, "he couldn't have."

Winnie thought she meant Josh. But Faith was looking at the TV. There was Faith, up on the Acting 101 stage, untying her braid, performing her seduction monologue. Boys in the crowd whistled and stomped their feet. Faith's face turned bright red. She buried her face in her hands.

"That Christopher's a creep," said Winnie, putting a comforting arm around her friend. The room grew silent as everyone became engrossed in Faith's performance. They applauded loudly when it ended.

"You were very good," said KC.

"Arrrgggghhhhhhh," said Faith. "I'm never going to survive this acting class."

Winnie searched the crowd with her eyes. She saw Josh leaning against a far wall. She knew he was still looking at her. The TV scene shifted and the bigger-than-life Liza Ruff appeared on the screen.

"This wasn't from class," said Faith.

Liza, fat pink hair rollers in her bright red hair, a torn bathrobe tied around her with rope, swung a little kid's sand pail filled with soap, toothpaste, and other bathroom goodies. She launched into a two minute comedy routine making fun of dorm food, roommates from hell, and love among the dormies. The crowd roared as she talked about the dining commons tuna surprise, trickling showers, and lack of privacy. She went on and on, but Winnie couldn't concentrate. Quietly, she got up from the sofa and walked through the dark room to where Josh stood, waiting.

"Hi," she said, softly.

"Hi yourself."

She wanted to reach out and touch him, but was afraid he'd pull away. She didn't feel she could take another rejection.

"I'm sorry—" they both said together.

"I didn't mean—" they said again. They laughed.

"You first," said Winnie.

"No, you go ahead." Behind them, the room rang with laughter at Liza's routine. But as far as Winnie and Josh were concerned, they were the only two people in the world.

"All right," said Winnie. She crossed her arms. "It's like this, Josh Gaffey. I want to be with you, but for some weird reason, every time we're about to get together, something happens to keep us apart."

"That's what *I* was going to say."

"And I'm beginning to wonder if maybe one of us doesn't really want to get together. If, maybe subconsciously, we're doing things on purpose so we can't get together."

"That's what *I* was going to say."

"And I think we're going to have to figure this

whole thing out because, I'll tell you right now, I can't go on like this."

"That's—"

"Will you stop interrupting!"

"It's hard to get a word in—"

"Half the time, I'm afraid I'll run into you in the dorm. The other half, I'm afraid I won't." Her motor-mouth was running full speed now, but she couldn't stop. It felt good to finally say all the things she'd been holding back. The problem was, she'd also started crying. She couldn't stop that, either.

"Sometimes I want to knock on your door and tell you how dumb all this fighting is. And other times I'm scared to death you'll knock on my door and say it's all over. Lately, I'm no good for anything or anyone, and I can't study and I keep bumping into walls and—"

Josh grabbed her and kissed her so hard their teeth clicked. Surprised, Winnie hesitated a second before she hugged him and kissed him right back. She held him as tight as she could. This time she wouldn't let go. This time they'd have to pry him out of her arms.

"All riiiight," someone yelled.

"Way to go!"

"It's about time."

Winnie and Josh looked up to the loud applause and whistles. They hadn't heard the newscast end, hadn't seen the lights come back on. They weren't aware of anything besides each other until the crowd circled around them and broke into a raucous round of applause.

"It's the Josh and Winnie Show," someone yelled.

Beaming, embarrassed, happy, Winnie and Josh turned to the crowd and, holding hands, took deep bows.

"Encore, encore," someone yelled.

"Later," Winnie and Josh said together. They laughed, arms around each other, as they led the procession into the dining room.

Eighteen

"My eyebrow pencil broke!"

"Here's a sharpener."

"Anybody seen my other shoe?"

"Under your chair."

"What time is it?"

"Seven-thirty."

The dancers raced around the backstage dressing room talking excitedly, doing their makeup, putting on costumes. Kimberly sat at the long makeup table, staring at herself in the dressing room mirror. Her face looked calm but her stomach was a mess, grumbling and growling with nerves.

She layered blue shadow heavily on her upper lid, then expertly stroked thick black eyeliner from the inner eye all the way up and out. The line would make her eyes appear exotic on stage, give them a cat-like slant. She drew red dots at the points of her eyes nearest the nose, to widen the eyes even more.

This will be over soon, she thought. *All of this.* Kimberly had come to a difficult but important decision. The end of her freshman year would also mark the end of her dancing profession. This afternoon, standing in front of that classroom full of eager young faces had touched something in her. Kimberly realized she wanted to explore other interests. She wasn't like the members of her mother's dance troupe who dedicated their lives and bodies to dance.

"You look terrific," said the dancer next to her. "Could you help me?"

"Sure." Kimberly studied the girl's coloring, then pulled a variety of pencils, brushes, and tubes out of her makeup box. "Tilt your head back and close your eyes." She'd had years of experience helping out backstage in Houston. She finished the eye makeup quickly and expertly. "Now, soften your lips," she said, outlining the girl's lips with a dark lipstick pencil. "That's good. Hold still." She used a lipstick to apply a lighter color inside.

"Isn't that too dark?" asked the girl. "I never wear lipstick."

"You need dark rouge and eyeshadow and lipstick on stage or the lights wash you out," said Kimberly. "Now blot." She handed the girl a tissue. The two of them looked in the mirror.

"I look older!" said the girl, admiring her dramatic new look. "Thanks."

Kimberly sat back down and opened the box of false lashes her mother had sent wrapped in a good luck card. "Break a leg" said the card. It was signed by the members of her mother's dance troupe. Knowing they were thinking of her back in Houston, wishing her luck, helped calm Kimberly's nerves. She knew professional dancers got the preperformance jitters, too. Kimberly was in good company.

Squeezing a thin line of glue along the back of the eye lashes, Kimberly blew on the glue a few seconds to help it set, then pressed the lashes into place.

"Flowers," called the stage manager, whisking into the dressing room. She pushed a cart full of flowers. "Christy. Meredith. Babe. Pearl. Connie." One by one she handed out flowers, mostly single roses, sent by the dancer's friends. "And these," she said, picking up a dozen long stem roses, "are for you." She handed them to Kimberly.

Kimberly stared. Long stem roses cost a fortune! Who would have sent these? She took the flowers and set them down on her makeup case. Her hands shook as she opened the card.

"For the world's greatest science teacher, and dancer, and lab partner . . . from the second greatest. Good luck tonight, Derek."

Derek! She turned the card over. On the back he'd written, "P.S. Just remember what you taught the kids, Action and Reaction. Dance is like physics and fencing and all those other things you're so good at. Break a leg. (My roommate says that means good luck on stage, but I don't see how. I think it sounds painful.)"

Kimberly pressed the card to her breast. Not only had Derek remembered her performance, he'd thought ahead far enough to order flowers. She laughed, feeling tears of joy creeping into her eyes. *Oh no!* she thought, blotting the tears with a tissue. *My false eyelashes will fall off.*

She closed her makeup box and set it aside. Derek was funny. She'd have to tell him that her mother had always told her that "Break a leg" referred to an actor "breaking" or "bending" a leg to take a bow. The idea was that if you performed well, the audience would applaud, and you would have to take a curtain call and "break" your leg. If your performance stank, no one would applaud, and you wouldn't have to take a bow. Kimberly wondered which she'd be doing, or not doing tonight.

"Does anyone have extra black tights?" cried a girl. "I just tore mine."

"Here." A pair of tights sailed across the room.

"Someone zip me up?"

"Where's the deodorant?"

"What time is it?"

"Seven forty-five."

"Oh no! I'll never be ready!"

Kimberly took her costume off the metal rack, slipped off her kimono, and began to dress. Thank goodness for this costume. Faith had gotten the idea for it at the fencing demonstration.

"You seemed able to forget the audience," Faith had said, "when you had that mask on. So maybe you just need a costume that will conceal your face in order to be less nervous."

Faith had scrounged through the theater arts costume department and found a full-length, black satin cape with a deep, dramatic hood. Kimberly had practiced her routine in the cape, loving how it fluttered and swirled, how it added drama and mystery. Most of all, she loved how it concealed her face.

"Ten minutes," said the stage manager. "Ten minutes, ladies."

"Oh, no!"

"Don't panic."

"Who has my scarf?"

Kimberly wanted to run or hide or catch the first bus to Mexico . . . anything but go on stage. She began to perspire. She dusted her body with powder and started tugging on the black, body-hugging cat suit.

"Five minutes," said the stage manager.

"You just said ten!"

"Five minutes to the first act."

Three girls next to Kimberly squealed, racing around, gathering props, brushing on more rouge, refreshing their lipstick. The performing arts department was filled with girls like these who lived to dance. They dreamed about careers in Broadway musicals and Hollywood movies. If only Kimberly had a passion for dance—for *something*. Maybe she'd go into math, or science, or teaching. So many interests pulled her in so many different directions. She was only seventeen years old.

Why was she expected to know what she wanted to do with the rest of her life?

"Safety pin!" wailed a girl. "Anyone have a safety pin? My snap broke."

"Here."

"You saved my life!"

The smell of Derek's roses made Kimberly smile. She always focused on one thing at a time, whether it was dance or fencing. Derek was probably too much the other way, not focusing on anything. Still, he made her understand that just because she was good at something didn't mean she had to make it her life's work.

"Time, ladies," called the stage director. "I need the first act in place, please."

The squealing trio left the dressing room and Kimberly worked the long sleeves of the cat suit up over her arms and onto her shoulders. In the distance, she heard the band strike up the opening music. She sat on the bench. It would be her turn all too soon.

Whatever happened out on that stage tonight, good or bad, she would tell her mother that she just wasn't cut out for a professional dance career. It wouldn't be easy, but it had to be done.

She stood, then threw her long, black cape over

her shoulders and joined the other performers in the wings.

The first few numbers went smoothly. The music cued up on time, the student dancers looked amazingly professional, and the audience was enthusiastic. Kimberly peeked out through the side curtain and saw Faith, Winnie, and KC sitting together in the fourth row. And Derek!

"Oh, no," she said, suddenly not sure she wanted him there. What if she fell or flubbed or—

The dance before hers ended, the performers ran off laughing, relieved, turning around to take one, then two bows. She could leave now. She could tell them to skip her number and go on to the next one. She didn't have to go on. She felt like her heart was going to beat its way out of her chest.

The theater lights went down and the audience grew silent. Kimberly swallowed as the music for her entrance began. She felt the mysterious chords flow into her, changing her from freshman Kimberly Dayton into the magical Merlin, the magician at midnight. Hunching her back, swirling her cape over and around, she took a deep breath and waited for the special effects technician to set off a burst of fire and a red cloud of smoke. As the audience gasped, Kimberly leapt through the smoke onto the stage.

She became Merlin, spinning spells, weaving magic. Kimberly wasn't *doing* a dance, she *was* the dance. The music was a part of her and the dance steps came as easily as breathing. She swirled the cape, leapt and twirled, moving her body like another strain of music. Finally, exhausted from a night of magic-making, she wrapped herself in the cape and, in another burst of fire and smoke, vanished from the stage.

"Bravo!"

"Yea!"

"More!"

The audience went wild, whistling, stomping, yelling. The other dancers pushed Kimberly back out for a bow. She "broke" her leg to the left, to the right, then bowed deeply toward her friends. Derek jumped to his feet, clapping and whistling.

Kimberly ran off, out of breath, laughing with relief and joy and something else—anticipation. Changes were happening in her life, good changes. She was going to give that big world out there a chance. She was going to taste all it had to offer.

Kimberly waited in the wings with the rest of the dancers until the concert ended. Then, holding hands, they all went out on stage for a final bow. Kimberly peered through the blinding lights, smiling at her friends. Derek's seat was empty! He'd left the concert. What now? A late night chemistry experiment? Sharpening his épée? She smiled at the audience, trying not to let her disappointment show.

Kimberly ran off stage with the other dancers, trying to adjust her eyes from the bright lights to the dark wings.

"Whoa!" Strong arms grabbed her around her waist, lifting her easily out of the line.

"Derek!"

He hugged her, spinning her around and around. "You were fantastic," he said. "Better than fantastic."

She laughed, hugging him back.

"Coming through," grumbled a stagehand, lugging huge cables.

Derek took Kimberly aside, then walked back through the hall filled with chattering performers and their friends.

"I see you remembered my performance," said Kimberly, stopping outside the dressing room door.

"Remembered it?" He brushed his thumb back

along her cheek. She shivered. "Hey, I even got here early."

"That must be a new record for you," she said. "What's the occasion?"

He held up a fist playfully, the same way she had in the classroom when she told him he'd better show up tonight. "I sure didn't want to find out what Kimberly Dayton's famous action-reaction was."

"Well, I'm honored you found the time to come," she teased, "knowing how busy your schedule is and all."

He arched an eyebrow. "I do take an occasional time-out," he said.

"Oh?"

"At least, I could. Maybe for a movie, or a walk along campus, or a boat ride on Mill Pond."

"Really?" She smiled, batting her long, false eyelashes at him.

"Yes," he said, slipping his arms around her, "really."

"That does sound interesting," said Kimberly. "Very, very interesting indeed."

She swirled the cape around her, covering them both from the noisy crowd. In the darkness inside the cape, she lifted her face to his, tasting the sweet warmth of his lips, feeling his heart beating in time with hers.

After a long while, they walked out of the theater, arm in arm, walking slowly back to the dorm. And even though Kimberly knew she had walked this way hundreds of times before, the path seemed suddenly unfamiliar and challenging. And all around her, the same old world looked miraculously fresh and new.

Here's a sneak preview of Freshman Rivals, *the twelfth book in the dramatic story of* FRESHMAN DORM.

"Aren't you ready yet?" Josh asked, poking his head inside Winnie's room. "It's almost seven o'clock. We'll never make it to meet your father at the restaurant on time at this rate."

"Let him wait," Winnie said, standing amid a pile of rejected outfits she'd tossed on the floor. "After sixteen years, a few more minutes shouldn't make a difference."

"Is that what you're wearing?" Josh asked, noticing Winnie's choice of a black T-shirt, black jeans, and plain white canvas sneakers. "It's not very festive."

Winnie shrugged as she pulled a faded denim jacket off its wire hanger in her closet. "We're not exactly going to Mardi Gras," she said. "Well, if we're going, let's go."

Winnie and Josh left Forest Hall and headed out into the starry night.

"You're in a great mood," Josh remarked sarcastically as they took a shortcut across the dorm green toward the parking lot. "I hope you're not going to act this way with your father."

Winnie knew she was behaving badly, but for some reason she couldn't stop herself. Maybe it was because, having agreed to meet her father again, she felt exposed and vulnerable. Now her father would probably think that she liked him, and he'd try to get closer to her. It didn't help that Josh was on her father's side.

"Just be glad I'm going at all," Winnie said sullenly. "It's more than he deserves."

They crossed Main Street and cut through a maze of alleyways. Emerging onto a side street, they reached a squat, brick building with ancient, crusted plate glass windows. A faded wooden sign over the door read *Hondo's Cafe*. Hondo's, home of the foot-long submarine sandwich, was U. of S.'s oldest and most popular hangout.

Winnie and Josh entered the brightly lit restaurant. The walls were lined with pennants and yellowing photographs of sports teams from Springfield's past. Sawdust covered the floor and the air was filled with happy chatter and vintage rock music from an old jukebox.

"Is that him?" Josh asked, pointing to a booth near the wooden counter where people stood on line to order their submarines.

Winnie glanced over to where Josh was pointing. Byron Jennings sat alone, nervously adjusting his red tie with yellow slashes running through it. He wore a crisp white shirt and a black and white houndstooth checked jacket. His slightly thinning dark hair was slicked straight back and his brown eyes flitted anxiously around the restaurant.

"Yes, that's him," Winnie said, taking a step back.

Byron spotted them and was instantly on his feet. "Hi, Winnie," he said, rushing to greet them. He leaned forward to kiss Winnie's cheek.

"Byron," Winnie said coldly, "this is my boyfriend, Josh Gaffey."

"Pleased to meet you," Byron said, vigorously shaking Josh's hand. "Come sit down. What would you like to eat? Anything you want, it's on me." Winnie ordered a meatball parmesan submarine and Josh ordered an Italian sub with french fries. "I'll be right back," Byron promised, scurrying to the counter to place their order.

"See," Josh said to Winnie as they sat next to each other on the wooden bench. "He's not so bad."

"Buying a couple of subs after never paying child support is hardly grounds for forgiveness," Winnie said sourly. "After everything my mother told me about him, he's lucky I'm even talking to him."

"Did you call your mother and tell her you heard from him?" Josh asked.

"Actually," Winnie said, "I haven't spoken to my mother yet. I figured it wasn't important enough to bother her with." Winnie ignored Josh as he rolled his eyes. "She's never described him in a particularly flattering way, you know."

"What way is that?"

"Lowlife. Infantile. Irresponsible. Flattering words like that."

"Maybe that's just her side of the story," Josh suggested. "Maybe she was really hurt by the divorce. Didn't you tell me, once, that he left her for another woman? That could explain why she's so bitter."

"Bon appetit, mes amis!" Byron said, bursting in on their conversation. He balanced a plastic tray loaded with food on one hand, and twirled an imaginary handlebar mustache with the other.

"We 'ave 'ere ze very delectable meatball sub avec fromage," he said in a convincing French accent, handing Winnie her meatball sub. "And, also, for ze gentleman, ze sub Italien, avec les pommes frites!" Byron unloaded Josh's plate along with two sodas in huge glasses that looked like fishbowls. He sat down across from Winnie and Josh, his own place empty.

"Aren't you eating anything?" Josh asked.

Byron shrugged. "I ate at the hotel," he said. "I'm really here to see Winnie, not to eat, although I will borrow a french fry." He leaned forward and grabbed a fat, greasy fry with his fingers.

"So," Josh said, looking from Winnie to Byron. "I guess you guys have a lot to talk about."

Winnie didn't bother to look up at Josh or her father. She just swirled her sub's melted cheese and tomato sauce with a plastic fork. She had nothing to say to her father, anyway. If he wanted to talk, it was up to him to say something.

"What brings you to town, Mr. Jennings?" Josh tried again.

"Call me Byron," Winnie's father said, plucking another french fry from Josh's paper container and munching while he talked. "Actually, Winnie is what brings me to town. I guess she told you that I haven't exactly been part of her life, so I understand completely why she'd rather look at tomato sauce than my ugly mug. I'm just grateful she's given me another chance to explain myself, although I have this feeling that you had something to do with it. I'm right, aren't I? You brought her here."

"Well . . ." Josh hemmed and hawed, "I didn't really."

"You're a sensitive young man, Josh," Byron said. "You've got heart. I can already see what Winnie sees in you. Hey, I know! I'll tell *you* my sob story, and if you buy any of it maybe you can put in a good word for me."

Josh laughed. *"I'm* willing to listen," he said, "and even if your adorable daughter *acts* like she's not, I'll bet she's listening too."

Winnie wanted to puke. Josh and her father had just met, and already they were acting like old friends.

Byron took a deep breath. "Okay," he said. "If I leave anything out, just ask Winnie to fill you in later tonight when she's yelling at you for being nice to me. Winnie's mother and I divorced when Winnie was two. It was . . . well . . . messy to put it mildly. But the thing I always wanted Winnie to understand was that I didn't divorce *her*. I wanted to see her, spend time with her, be a dad to her, but her mother wouldn't let me anywhere near her. Part of the divorce settlement was that Francine had full custody, and no matter how many times I called, she wouldn't even let me come for a visit."

Fragments of late-night conversations Winnie hadn't even remembered she'd heard suddenly came back to her. *Byron, I said no! It's for her own good, and you know what I'm talking about . . . It isn't fair to raise her hopes that way. You'll just disappoint her . . .* Winnie couldn't have been more than four or five years old when she'd heard her mother's muffled voice from the living room at an hour when she should have been asleep.

"Not that I blame Fran one bit," Byron continued, drumming his fingers on the table. "I remarried very soon after the divorce and I'm sure she resented me for that. I moved to Denver and started my own business which was quite successful. I wanted to send money for Winnie, but Francine didn't want anything to do with me. My new wife, too, was very possessive and wanted me all to herself, so that made it even harder for me to be with my daughter. After a few more years went by, I finally stopped trying. Maybe I should never have given up, I don't know."

"It sounds like you tried pretty hard," Josh said,

opening his mouth wide to get it around his tall sandwich.

Winnie bit the end of her straw. Why hadn't her mother mentioned any of this? When Winnie had asked where her father was, all her mother had said was that she'd be better off not knowing. Didn't she think Winnie would have wanted to know that her father was trying to get in touch with her?

On the other hand, Winnie trusted her mother's judgment. If her mother had tried that hard to prevent her from seeing her father, she must have had a good reason. The only problem was, Winnie couldn't see what that reason was. All she could see, so far, was a guy who was trying very hard to make her like him.

"There's one thing I don't understand," Josh said, washing down his sub with a sip of cola. "Why now? Why did you come looking for Winnie after all these years?"

Winnie was grateful to Josh for asking all these questions. She really *was* curious to know more, even if she didn't want her father to know that.

Byron sighed and leaned back against the dark wooden bench. "I'm a two-time loser," he said. "My second marriage just ended. I won't even go into that. You might say I'm at a juncture in my life. Winnie's the only family I've got. And I knew she would be eighteen. She's legally an adult and can make her own decision whether or not she wants to know me."

That was exactly what Winnie had just been thinking. The more she reflected on what her mother had done, the angrier she became. It really wasn't fair that her mother had denied her an opportunity to know the only father she'd ever have. Even if her father was as bad as her mother said, didn't Winnie have the right to draw her own conclusions?

"Can we please stop talking about me in the third person?" Winnie demanded, finally looking up and catching her father's eye.

"She speaks!" Byron declared happily, doing a little tap dance under the table.

"I knew she'd come around," Josh said, wrapping his arm around Winnie's shoulder and squeezing her.

"Does this mean I'm forgiven?" Byron asked, his face filled with hope.